Who is this menacing woman and why does Teddy feel so threatened by her?

Teddy glanced at the woman. She stood a little shorter than Teddy, and somewhat heavier. Her dark blonde hair, straggling to her shoulders, looked as though it had never been washed. Too much dark blue makeup surrounded pale blue eyes, and oversized glasses hid much of her face.

Her bright red lips opened to reveal darkly stained teeth. "Well, don't you know who owns this dump?" The woman practically spat the harsh words at Teddy.

Teddy nodded. "It's the Marland ranch."

The woman's pale eyes swept the yard and nearby area. "Well, where's the old lady?"

Teddy began to feel uneasy. This could be anyone.

VERALEE WIGGINS is the author of more than ten novels, including *A Rose for Bethany* and *April Showers*. Ms. Wiggins makes her home in Washington State.

Llama
Lady

VeraLee Wiggins

Heartsong Presents

ISBN 1-55748-363-9

LLAMA LADY

PRINTED IN U.S.A.

one

The savage attack on the front door caused Teddy Marland to do more than drop a stitch—the entire sweater flew from her grasp. She checked the clock; it was only half past six in the morning. Gram had just put breakfast on the table and she had just picked up her knitting after having finished feeding and watering the livestock.

"Lord, grant me patience with the fool who's on the other side of this opening," she prayed, heading for the door that seemed about to crumble under yet another brutal attack. Jerking open the door she discovered a huge blond man with his right arm raised and ready to administer still another round of battery. His face looked like one of the thunderstorms common to Bend, Oregon—one of the bad ones.

Teddy stood tall in the doorway. "What do you think you're doing?" she asked.

The stranger, with his large hand still suspended in air, looked at Teddy, and looked some more. His craggy face began to relax, then his mouth tightened again. "Get the owner of this zoo!"

Teddy started to yell for Gram, but the tiny woman had already scurried in from the kitchen and was now wiping her hands on the sides of her pants. Rushing to Teddy's side, Gram snaked her skinny arm around Teddy's slim waist which was about even with the old woman's shoulder. "All right, buster," she announced in a gravelly voice that was bigger than she, "we've had it up to here with your tantrum. If you want something, ask like a gentleman. Otherwise get

5

on down the road."

The man's mouth slackened; his eyes darted from Teddy down to Gram and back up to Teddy again. Then the corners of his mouth began jerking, and a low belly laugh rumbled from somewhere deep within.

"Well, can we help you, or did you just have the urge to destroy our house?" Gram's guttural voice demanded.

"Did anyone ever tell you two that you make a crazy looking pair?" he finally asked.

"Is that a fact?" Gram replied, peering up at the man from her four-foot, eleven-inch frame. "Well, you have one up on us. It doesn't take two of you to look crazy."

The man stood silent, his shoulders still shaking.

Teddy looked at Gram who was her mother, father, and entire family, rolled into one tiny dynamo. Why would they look crazy together? True, the top of Gram's yellow-gray head was several inches short of reaching Teddy's shoulder, and Gram looked so thin she might not cast a shadow. But she still appeared beautiful to Teddy, even in her size ten, boys' bib overalls and red-plaid flannel shirt. Then Teddy looked down at her own worn jeans and faded tee shirt and realized she did not look too gorgeous either. But crazy?

The tall man returned to life, possibly remembering why he came. His lips tightened again; red streaks brightened his already sunburned skin and his eyes blazed. "I asked for the owner of this spread," he told Gram, tersely.

Gram straightened her shoulders and stood tall. She tightened her grip on Teddy's waist. "You're looking at 'em." Her voice sounded like a gravel crusher.

He pulled out a scrap of paper, checked it, wadded it in his hand and shoved it back into his jeans pocket. "The mailbox says Theodore Marland."

Gram jabbed a bony thumb toward Teddy. "That's Theodore Marland. You got a problem with that?"

The man considered a moment. "No," he said firmly, "I don't have a problem with, uh, her. But I want to talk to a man."

"Well, you won't find one of those around this place." Gram leaned back, looking up into his face. Then she smiled, and her faded blue eyes crinkled. "Come on, sonny, you got a problem, tell me. Maybe I can fix it."

After a moment of indecision, he spoke. "How many times a week are you supposed to get water?"

Gram jerked her old head up at him. "Who, may I ask, are you?"

"I'm Brandon Sinclair. I bought the ranch just west of here, and I was told that this is my water day."

Gram turned her back and headed for the kitchen. "I don't have time to spoon-feed every greenhorn who comes along," she grated over her shoulder. "If you'll help the fool figure out his water problems, Teddy, I'll hold breakfast for fifteen minutes."

Teddy sighed and stepped onto the rickety porch. "Come on out and I'll show you how it works." She closed the door and stepped gingerly down the rotting steps. "I don't understand how you could mess up your water. You're the last one on the line."

"I may be a greenhorn," he bellowed, "and I may also be a fool, but even I can see that you're taking my water!"

Teddy did not not respond as he followed her across her overgrown yard through the gate and into the pasture. Llamas appeared from several directions and followed the two across the pasture, their heads resting on Teddy's or Mr. Sinclair's shoulders. Other llamas, in their eagerness to be with her, bumped into Teddy.

"And why are you raising these, uh, goats?" he shouted.

"I'm not deaf," she said quietly, striding beside him. "And I'm sure you know they're llamas. We raise them because we make several times the money with them that we did raising cattle. And we have a lot more fun doing it."

In a few minutes they reached a bubbling stream about three feet wide and two feet deep. As they continued to walk across the pasture, Teddy explained how the Deschutes County ranchers shared the water. "The water comes from the Deschutes River and is divided into many lines so each rancher gets enough to survive but not a lot more than that. A line is simply a wide ditch with lots of water flowing through it. There is one ranch before mine on this particular line, and you are the last. We each get water twice a week. None comes through on Sunday. The first ranch gets water on Monday and Thursday, I get it Tuesday and Friday, and you get it Wednesday and Saturday."

"I know all that. Is this Wednesday?" he asked, obviously struggling for civility.

"This is Wednesday and you're getting the water." She glanced at the rushing water again. "You can see there's plenty in the ditch."

They approached the gates and Teddy could not believe her eyes. Water gushed through her open gate, into her nearly filled pond! She pushed the lever that closed her gate and sent the water coursing through his ditch into his nearly dry pond.

Her bright blue eyes looked into his, laughing at him. "I don't know how you bumbled the gate open, but I closed it this morning. I always do it at exactly six o'clock, the shut-off time."

"How could I bumble?" he shouted. "I don't even have a gate; I get water when no one else wants it."

Even though Brandon Sinclair stood there accusing her of stealing his water, Teddy's kind heart went out to the frenzied man. "No one's stealing your water, Mr. Sinclair," she said softly. "Ranchers work together. We not only share water, but anything else the other person needs. You go on back to your own place now, and things will be all right."

As Teddy watched her new neighbor trot to the old log fence and jump over, she wished she could have met him under more favorable circumstances. She had never seen such an attractive man. His shoulders were wide and his legs went on forever. And his sun-streaked blond hair and bright brown eyes could really do something to a girl. Wait a minute! What was she thinking about, anyway? She was not shopping for a man.

When Teddy crossed her unstable porch floor again, she wondered for the hundredth time how soon they would be able to repair the old house. They had mortgaged the ranch to buy the llamas and all repairs had been put on hold until the loan could be paid off. She opened the door, removed her shoes, ran through the completely empty living room to the bathroom to wash up, then slipped into her chair at the kitchen table.

Gram asked the blessing then poured coffee into fat brown mugs. "Well, did you get him calmed down?"

Teddy shook her head. "I don't know, he's pretty upset." She took a sip of the delicious liquid. "I tried to explain about the water. But our gate *was* open. I told him he must have done it. I remember closing it after I finished the chores."

Gram nodded. "Wonder what he's doing on a ranch. Looks as if he wouldn't know which end of a cow to feed."

Teddy and Gram finished breakfast and stacked the dishes

in the sink. Then they hurried across the pasture to set up the irrigation system in the alfalfa. They would use up what water they had left from yesterday then start all over again on Friday. The fifty-acre alfalfa field provided enough hay to keep their llamas through the winter.

They barely had four of their eight monstrous water gun sprinklers set up when a horse and rider pounded up to them. He jumped from the saddle, marched up to Teddy, and leaned over her, his face contorted. "Do you really want the water or are you just trying to make me crazy?" Brandon Sinclair yelled.

"Are you sure the gate's open again? If it is, it must be faulty," Teddy said trying to keep *her* voice calm.

Sinclair put his hands around Teddy's waist, hoisted her onto his horse, then hopped up into the saddle. "We'll see what's faulty," he informed her.

When they reached the water gate, Brandon Sinclair rolled off his horse and jerked Teddy down beside him. The curious llamas surrounded them as they walked toward the wide open irrigation gate.

Almost before he could point at the unobstructed water gushing toward her pond, Teddy pushed the lever and the gate instantly swung shut. "It seems to work just fine," she said, determined to keep calm.

"You bet it works! And if this happens again, I'm reporting you to the water master!"

Teddy felt her patience growing taut. "Mr. Sinclair," she said, a little louder than necessary, "no one around here steals water or anything else for that matter. I'd be much more likely to share my water with you than to steal yours."

"Glad to hear it. Just the same, you'd better remember I'm watching my water as if it were diamonds rolling through that gate." He jumped on his horse.

At that moment, a beautiful cream and dark brown llama named Iris walked up, took the lever in her mouth and pulled back. The gate opened and the water once again rushed into the Marland line.

"Iris! What did you do?" Teddy pushed the lever, even as she yelled at the llama. "Did you see that?" she said, looking up, wide-eyed, at the man astride the horse.

Brandon Sinclair dismounted. "I wouldn't have believed it if I hadn't seen it. How long have you had her trained to do that?"

"Don't be ridiculous. I suppose she did it because she sees me doing it all the time."

The tall man remained silent a moment, then laughed out loud and climbed back onto his horse. "Sorry I accused you of stealing my water," he called, starting back toward his own ranch. A moment later he stopped short. "The problem is located, but not corrected," he yelled across the distance.

"I'll think of something," she mumbled as she watched him gallop back to his own ranch. She walked away slowly with her arm around the animal's neck. "Come on, Iris, you have to stay in the small corral until we get this figured out."

The next afternoon Teddy hauled fence posts and wire out to the irrigation line to build a fence and gate to keep Iris away from the water gate. Working in the warm June sunshine, she dug four post holes, buried the posts, and started unrolling the wire fencing.

"Think that'll do it?"

Teddy turned at the sound of the warm deep voice to find Brandon Sinclair standing, feet apart, watching her work. "I hope so," she replied. "Iris is so mad at me for penning her up that she won't even look at me."

Sinclair took the wire from her hands. "Here, let me help. I'm probably a little stronger than you." They worked together until the fence protected the water gate from the llamas.

"I understand what a cattle ranch is all about," Brandon said, "but how do these things make you money? You don't eat them, do you?"

Teddy reached her arm around a long woolly neck. "Never. Don't talk like that in front of my girls. How do llamas make money? Well, the wool is worth two dollars an ounce, as compared to one dollar a pound for sheep wool. Llama wool is much stronger, warmer, and comes in many beautiful natural colors. A llama produces around five pounds of wool a year. Our herd numbers around 500 right now. Are you doing your arithmetic?"

Brandon's eyes grew round. "If you're telling me you take in $80,000 a year on llama wool, then I'm getting rid of my cattle tonight."

Teddy laughed. "I'm telling you we could. And some people do. But we don't shear our llamas. We sell the young. We get $10,000 to $15,000, and sometimes more, for females, and $1,000 or more for males. People buy them before they're born and take them when they're weaned, at about six months. We sell about 200 young each year, and so far we've been having slightly more females than males. Now, Mr. Sinclair, it's my turn to ask some questions."

"Brand. My friends call me Brand." He looked down at her, a soft friendly look replacing the anger. The sun sent gold flecks skittering around in his eyes.

"All right, Brand. How long have you been ranching beside us?" Teddy looked west to the shining white fences, the monstrous white barns, and metal loafing sheds. The three-story, white colonial house stood on a small knoll, overlooking the ultra-modern ranch. She knew it had been empty for the last six months since the old rancher had died.

"Arrived on the scene early this week. I'm still getting it set up."

"Where are you from?" The llamas jostled the two as they walked along, often distracting them from their discussion.

Brand shoved a large black llama away. "I'm from Alvadore, near Eugene. Western Oregon, you know? My folks had a large ranch there but they retired and moved into Eugene. I'd helped them from the time I was a child so ranching is in my blood." He held his arm out and up and shoved the llamas away again.

"Why Bend? Why did you buy in our area?"

He smiled. "I've always liked Bend. It's such a nice clean little town." He shoved two woolly heads away, then grinned, almost embarrassed. "And I suppose the fact that you can buy a lot more ranch here, for the same money, may have influenced me some."

One extra large red and white llama insisted on hanging its head over Brand's shoulder, so Brand gave it a mighty shove. The llama stepped back a few feet from Brand, raised its head as high as it could, laid back its ears, and began chewing vigorously. "No, Casanova, no!" Teddy yelled, but she hardly had the words out of her mouth when the llama let loose a great green missile which found its mark, splattering all over Brand's face.

two

Brand's hands flew to his face, his fingers clawing the horrible stuff away. As the stench filled her nostrils, Teddy's stomach threatened to turn. When Brand was able to see, he ran to the irrigation ditch, dropped to his stomach and splashed innumerable handfuls of water on his face. Then he sat down in the grassy pasture and looked up at Teddy. "What was that?" he implored.

"I guess I forgot to tell you that llamas spit when they get really upset. You shoved Casanova one too many times."

"Oh." Brand turned his hands over, looking at them as though they might fall off at any moment. "I'm not sure I want to know, but what do they spit?"

"It's half-digested food."

"I'm keeping my cattle, after all. I knew there had to be a catch."

That night Teddy told Gram about Brand helping her fix the fence and also about Casanova spitting on the poor man. "Teddy, when you talk about Brand, you have a new sparkle in your eyes," Gram said after they had finished laughing.

"No way," Teddy replied.

Gram nodded her wise old head. "All right. Just take my advice and don't mention Brandon Sinclair to Lynden."

A quiet tap on the door ended the discussion about Teddy's new sparkle. Lynden Greeley, Teddy's boyfriend since high school, stepped into the large bare room. The thin, brown-haired young man left his shoes at the front door, moved through the bare living room to the bathroom to wash his hands, then went to the cozily furnished country kitchen. Settling into the worn but comfortable couch, he glanced at Teddy. "Why the sparkle in those big blue eyes tonight?" he asked, absent-mindedly stroking Thor, the old yellow cat, who had climbed onto his lap.

When Lynden said "sparkle," Teddy's bright eyes flew to Gram's faded ones. She made up her mind never to think about Brandon Sinclair again in her entire life. "Anything exciting happen today?" she asked. Lynden worked at the *Bulletin*, Bend's daily newspaper, and Teddy thought he learned something new and stimulating every day.

Lynden shrugged and reached into the candy dish for some jellybeans. "No, we can hardly find anything to fill the local pages." He grinned at Teddy. "What do you expect from our nice quiet little town?"

"Young man," Gram said, interrupting the conversation, "you know I don't mind your eating that candy and I don't mind your petting the cat, either. But not at the same time in my house. Don't you dare stick your hand back into the candy dish until you go wash it with soap and water."

Lynden pushed the cat onto the couch, obediently went to the kitchen sink to wash his hands, then returned and sat down.

"What do you want to do tonight?" she asked.

"I'm awfully comfortable. How about watching TV?"

"Sure." She flipped the switch. "Mind if I knit then?"

He nodded. "Whatever makes you happy."

Sunday morning, Lynden Greeley called for Teddy and Gram at exactly quarter past nine, as he always did, to take them to church. "You look lovely," he told Teddy, as he

helped her into the back seat of his compact car. "I especially
like the light green suit you're wearing. You knitted that last
year, didn't you?" Then he turned his attention to Gram and
helped her into the front seat.

When they walked into the small white community
church, Teddy gulped. Brand Sinclair sat on the far end of the
last row of pews. After a moment of staring, she followed
Gram and Lynden to their usual seat on the aisle, half way
down. Teddy barely heard the sermon; she was so aware of
the big man sitting in the back of the church. To make matters
worse, she felt he was staring at her during the entire service.

After church, the members of the small congregation
lingered in the warm sunshine, visiting. Eventually, Brand
greeted Teddy and she introduced him to Lynden.

"Anyone invite you home for lunch?" Gram asked in her
usual brusque style.

Brand shook his sunshiny hair and his brown eyes danced.
"Not yet, Mrs. Marland, but I'm still hoping."

"Nelle," Gram said. "Call me Nelle. Why don't you come
on over to our place? You already know where it is, and you
won't have far to go home."

"Well, Nellie—"

"Nelle, sonny, not Nellie. All right, we'll see you in a little
while. Don't be too long, because our meal is all ready. You
know the commandments, I suppose."

When they got home, Teddy changed her clothes in a
hurry so she could help Gram with the food. They had it
steaming on the table when Brand joined them.

"Leave your shoes at the door and wash your hands in the
bathroom," Gram barked when Brand stepped inside. "Shoes
are filthy things."

One golden eyebrow rose, but he said not a word as he

stepped out of his boots and strode through the empty living room to the bathroom to comply. When he returned, he hesitated, looking the table over.

"Well, sit down there by Teddy," Gram commanded but Lynden dropped into the chair. Gram waggled a finger at Brand. "You can sit by me, then. I'm almost as good company as Teddy, don't you think?"

Brand sat down beside the tiny shriveled woman and took her hand. "Sure, Gram, you're all right."

"Nelle, sonny." Her old eyes spun over the young faces around her. "Everybody's hands still clean?"

Lynden and Teddy nodded. Brand looked at his, front and back. He nodded, too.

"All right, I guess you're the guest, Brand, so you just go ahead and ask the blessing."

"Look, Gram," Brand said, "I don't know any blessings except 'God is Great.' You don't want that, do you?"

Lynden cleared his throat and prayed a prayer so long that Teddy knew for sure the chicken would be cold. She peeked to see if he was about to wind down, and met Brand's golden gaze. He winked at her, then closed both eyes tight. Teddy closed hers, too.

After the meal everyone sat down on the couch, love seat, and rocking chair to visit. "What did you do before coming here, Sinclair?" Lynden wanted to know.

"Helped my folks on their ranch," Brand answered willingly and then he invited them all to see his ranch. "It doesn't have anything exotic, like Teddy's goats," he joked, "but I'd like to show you anyway."

"I've been wanting to get a good look at that fancy place," Teddy said.

"You two run along," Gram said. "Lynden and I'll stay

here and see if we can eat all the candy."

Brand and Teddy jumped to their feet and Lynden raised himself half off the couch, then settled back down. "Don't be gone too long," he said, unwrapping a small candy bar.

In their eagerness to be off, Brand and Teddy literally ran off the porch but, when they stepped through the yard gate, the llamas surrounded them and forced them to slow down.

"Are we in danger?" Brand asked.

"No. Casanova is the only one that spits and you're the third person he's spit on. But I'll call the dogs." She stuck two fingers into her mouth and let out a whistle that almost knocked her own ears out of her head. A moment later, two gray and white dogs appeared. Teddy made a sweeping motion with her arm. "Take them back there," she said softly.

The dogs quietly went to work and, in a few minutes, they had herded the llamas to the back side of the pasture.

"Wow!" Brand said. "Those dogs are worth more than the llamas."

Teddy shook her head. "No, but they're worth a lot."

"Who's that jerk who ate lunch with us?" Brand asked as they walked across the pasture toward his place.

Teddy smiled. "That _jerk_ is my boyfriend. We've been going together for a long time."

Brand shook his head but said nothing more about Lynden. "How come your grandmother wears boys' jeans to church?" he asked.

Teddy laughed out loud. "She wears boys' clothes everywhere, hadn't you noticed? She's pretty tiny and they seem to fit."

"Yes, but to church?"

Teddy's blue eyes flashed mischievously. "She does dress up for church. She wears jeans to church rather than bib overalls, and tee shirts rather than flannel. And besides that she wears newer sneakers."

"Okay, I can handle that. How come you live with her?"

"Who else would I live with? I'm not married or anything, and we work the ranch together."

They came to the border fence—a rotted, falling-down, log fence. Brand looked the fence over as he helped Teddy across, but said nothing. "What about your folks?" he asked when they were on their way again.

Teddy's cheeks burned. He had asked the one question she could not handle. "I don't have any folks except Gram," she snapped in a voice that brooked no further discussion. "Gramp died just before I was born."

"Okay, one more question. Whose ranch is it?" His eyes asked Teddy if that question was okay, and she smiled.

"Legally, it's mine," she answered. "Gram insisted on putting it in my name when I turned twenty-one. But really, it belongs to both of us."

Brand stopped walking and turned to face Teddy. "How old are you?"

"Twenty-one on my last birthday. Why does that surprise you?"

"Well, I thought you were a kid, maybe sixteen."

They started walking across his pasture, toward the neat, modern buildings scattered over the huge place.

"My turn," Teddy said, laughing. "I have to know why you said Gram and I made a crazy-looking pair."

Brand turned amused eyes on her. "It looked like a mouse defending an elephant."

"Cute! Really cute. Of course, there's no question who the elephant was, is there?"

Brand moved to Teddy's side and dropped a long, sun-tanned arm across her shoulders. "You're a graceful willowy girl, Teddy, and I'm sure you're well aware of just how beautiful you are. I've never seen such soft, shiny hair, and the gold highlighting the dark color is nothing less than spectacular. And your shockingly blue eyes are entrancing. But. . . . Have you ever seen anyone as tiny as your grandmother in your entire life?"

Teddy laughed and moved away from Brand, causing his hand to crash to his side. "I guess I'm used to her," she said. "She's just right to me."

When he was finished showing Teddy around the ranch, Brand suggested they look at the inside of the house.

"I better not go inside," she said hesitantly.

"Twenty-one's old enough to go into a neighbor's house," Brand said. "Anyway, we won't be alone." He took her arm and led her through the yard, which Teddy noticed was immaculately weeded and trimmed, unlike her own jungle.

"Hannah, Rolf," Brand called when the front door closed behind them. The house must have been about 150 years newer than hers. Thick, cream-colored carpets covered the wide expanse of floor and modern paintings hung in exactly the right places on sparkling white walls.

She followed him through a large dining room, into a kitchen, the likes of which Teddy had never seen.

"We're here, Brand," a voice called from somewhere, and a middle-aged couple appeared through a door.

Brand smiled. "Rolf, Hannah, this is our next-ranch neighbor, Teddy Marland. Teddy, these are the people who take care of the place and me. Especially me. The Perrys, Rolf and Hannah."

Hannah, probably in her early fifties, red-headed, freckled, and large, shook Teddy's hand, then dropped it and hugged her. "We're glad to know you at last," she said.

Rolf, a little older and with gray hair, took Teddy's hand and pumped it vigorously. "Yes, at last."

After a few minutes of visiting, Brand invited Teddy to see the stables.

"What was that 'we're meeting you at last,' stuff?" Teddy asked as they walked through the equally well kept back yard. "Have they been here a long time?"

Brand grinned foolishly and shook his head. "No, they came from Alvadore with me. I may have mentioned your name a couple of times," he confessed at Teddy's raised eyebrows. then he opened the stable door, motioning Teddy in. "Let me introduce you to our horses. This is Misty. She's a real lady. Spicy, but sweet." Teddy took in the sleek palomino mare.

"And this is Thunder. You probably recognize him from my crazy ride to your place. Thunder is my special stallion. He can always give me more than I bargain for." Teddy looked up at the huge black stallion. She had no doubt he would be more than she could handle.

Brand showed her the two other horses, a large chestnut gelding, Pharaoh, and Powder, a fat dark mare.

Teddy turned glowing blue eyes to Brand. "I love them. We don't have any horses and I've always wanted some."

"Want to take a ride?"

"I'd love to . . . if you'll be patient with a greenhorn and a fool besides."

Brand saddled Thunder and Misty and helped Teddy onto Misty, who pranced daintily in one spot, eager to be off.

They walked around the pasture for a little while, then Brand trotted Thunder and Misty followed. "Want to ride over to your place and show Gram the horses?"

"Yes! Let's do. But she wants you to call her Nelle."

As they approached the house, Teddy mentally compared her home to Brand's. Half as large and all on one floor, its sides were made of weathered logs. The wooden windows looked old and worn. And the inside! She would rather not even think about that right now. Her eyes lifted to the bright blue tile roof. Such a fancy roof looked silly on the decrepit old house, but Gram said if they always repaired it with good material, one day the house would look great. Teddy was not so sure about that.

Teddy nimbly slid off the friendly little palomino's back and sprinted toward the old house. He followed her up the rickety steps. Both carefully skirted the most severely rotted area. They laughed together at the sheer delight of the afternoon. Suddenly, the door burst open and Lynden stood in the opening. He was not laughing.

three

The laughter slowly died to a stiff silence. "Do you realize you've been gone over two hours, Teddy?" Lynden asked in a stern voice.

"No!" Teddy said with a little gasp. "I completely lost track of the time."

"Time passes quickly when you're having fun," Brand quipped.

"Butt out, cowboy," Lynden snapped. Returning his attention to Teddy, he spoke roughly, scolding. "We planned to go to a concert in Pioneer Park this afternoon."

"I forgot all about it. Is it too late?" Teddy felt breathless for some strange reason . . . and guilty.

"Of course it's too late. It's nearly over."

Brand took Teddy's upper arm in his fingers. "Good, let's get a drink of water and ride some more."

Lynden knocked Brand's hand from Teddy's arm and jerked her away. "Not so fast, big shot, she's staying with me."

Brand's golden brown eyes burned into Teddy's. "Teddy?"

"Oh, I don't know," she said. "I should stay with Lynden. But I should take Misty back, too."

"Don't give it another thought," Brand said. He turned to go, then faced Teddy again. "Where's Gram?" he asked.

"Out making sure the llamas have plenty of food and water," Lynden replied.

"And you didn't go help?" Brand asked. "Will you tell Gram thanks for the fantastic meal?" he said to Teddy. "See you later."

"Where does he get off, calling Nelle, Gram?" Lynden asked.

Teddy shook her weary head. "I don't know. I just don't know." She felt as though the sun had disappeared behind a black cloud. Stepping into the living room, she listlessly pulled off her boots. Lynden followed.

Just then Gram came in, singing a hymn at the top of her voice. "Everyone out there's fat and happy," she announced at the end of the lively chorus.

"I'm sorry, Gram," Teddy said, "I didn't realize how late it is."

Gram made a silent "Pooh." Teddy thought her grandmother's old eyes had a special glint in them. "Who keeps track of time on Sunday?" Gram added. "I was glad for the exercise and it didn't take a minute. Brand came out to help, but I was finished. I noticed he led the palomino back home. I hope you didn't get hurt."

"No, I decided to stay here with Lynden."

"Oh? He decide to do something? The candy must be gone."

Teddy glanced at the empty candy dish. "What would you like to do, Lynden, go for a ride?"

"What's to see? Another mile out and there's nothing but sagebrush."

"Should we go to Pioneer Park? It's shady and pleasant."

"What's the matter with here? It's shady and pleasant here, too, isn't it?"

Lynden stayed for supper but never quite recovered from Teddy's neglect through the rest of the afternoon.

After Teddy went to bed that night a big, windblown figure galloped around in her head, astride an enormous black stallion. "This is ridiculous," she told herself and asked the Lord to help her empty her mind and fall asleep. He did.

"You look as if you need another two hours' sleep," Gram announced cheerfully the next morning when Teddy slid into her chair.

"I'm all right, Gram, I just need my coffee."

Gram filled a fat brown mug with the steaming liquid and slapped it down beside Teddy's plate. "What're we doing today, kitten?"

"Moving the herd to the north pasture. After that, we could go through and knock out the big weeds. As scarce as water is, I can't stand feeding and watering weeds."

"Sounds good. I'll be out before you finish moving the llamas."

Teddy's eyes gazed toward the west as she opened the gate between the two pastures, then she walked out to the llamas. She hoped she would run into Brand today. He had not seemed bothered when she decided to stay with Lynden, but why should he? They were barely friends and she had told him right off that Lynden was her boyfriend.

Teddy looked around at the llamas, all walking or running toward her, the babies keeping near their mothers. She stuck her fingers into her mouth and whistled. The dogs appeared, trotting casually to her. "Hi, Brutus, Caesar," she greeted them. "Okay, guys, take us to the north pasture, but real easy."

Teddy began walking north with llamas surrounding her. Casanova and Iris crowded so close they bumped against her as they walked. The dogs separated, one to the east, one to the west, and trotted casually back and forth, keeping the llamas in a fairly tight group. "Great going, guys," Teddy called to the dogs.

Then Casanova stiffened, and his ears flapped back against his head. Teddy turned to find Brand about fifty feet behind her. "Don't come any closer," she called softly. "We'll have these guys put away in a few minutes, then I'll join you."

She locked the gate that connected the south and north pastures and returned to Brand. "Now, what can I do for you?" she asked with a welcoming smile.

"I didn't want anything, especially. I saw the dogs working the little camels and thought I'd watch. Why did you stop me? Afraid I'd stampede the buffalo?"

She grinned. "I did it for your own protection. You seem to have made an enemy among my flock."

He looked surprised. "I didn't see Lynden anywhere."

Teddy chuckled. "Maybe you made more than one enemy, come to think of it. I meant Casanova. You remember him?"

He nodded and grinned. "Oh yes. The dirty bird that spit on me! Believe me, I'll give him plenty of clearance from now on."

"Want to sit down a minute?" Teddy asked.

"Here?" He looked around the grassy pasture. "Sure as I sit down, I'll find a llama pie."

Teddy shook her head. "No way. Llamas all go to one corner. Not only does it keep the pasture clean, but it makes fertilizing the garden awfully easy. Now, back to your problem with my friend, Casanova," she said mischievously. "He remembers you and evidently the memory isn't pleasant. Before llamas spit, they tense up, their ears flatten and they start chewing. He saw you before I did and alerted me. I noticed his head go up. He would have spit if you'd kept coming."

Brand grinned. "He's just jealous. So's your other friend

for that matter."

Teddy pulled up her knees and put her arms around them. "I don't think Lynden's jealous. I haven't given him any reason to be."

"He has reason to be jealous of anyone who lives and breathes and moves. Now, to change the subject, why don't you tell me about yourself," Brand suggested. "Where did you go to college?"

College? Teddy had been so busy with the ranch she had not even thought about college. Now she felt embarrassed to admit it. "Nowhere," she finally said, softly. "I suppose you went to some fancy school?"

He shook his head. "Nope. I went to Oregon State University. Majored in business administration and animal husbandry. Ranching, I guess you'd call it."

"So . . . we're going to watch a rancher who does it by the book," she replied.

Hearing a buzzing noise like a million extra-loud bees, they looked up to see Gram pile off her motorcycle. "Hey, is this the way you're getting the work done?" the old lady called in her guttural voice. But, as she trotted nearer, Teddy noticed a definite gleam in her faded eyes. Either the old lady was kidding or she had a crush on Brand.

"Sit down a minute and catch your breath," Brand said, patting a spot beside him.

"Brand's just telling me about his college education," Teddy said.

"And Teddy's telling me she hasn't had hers yet," Brand added.

"Oh, she's educated," Gram said. "She graduated from the college of hard knocks with a master's degree in Good Judgment from Bad Experience. She's also taken many

classes in gaining good experience from bad judgment."
Then she said, "I have to get busy. You two can waste this
gorgeous day if you want to." She kicked the motorcycle to
life and tore off toward the house. A few minutes later she
started across the pasture on foot, whacking away at the
weeds with her sharp hoe.

"I have one more question," Brand said. "Is your name
really Theodore?"

Teddy's eyes smiled, though her mouth remained still.
"That's my name."

"Why?"

Teddy shrugged. "I guess Gram liked it. Maybe she didn't
know it was a boy's name."

"Gram. Always Gram. Is she really your mother?"

This time Teddy did smile. "I'm twenty-one, she's sev-
enty-eight. Does that tell you anything?"

He looked into Teddy's blue eyes with curiosity. "Grand-
mothers usually don't name their grandchildren," he said
softly.

Ugh. If she could just learn to keep her mouth shut every
discussion might not turn to her origins. Why did everyone
have to be so nosy, anyway? Thank goodness Lynden had
never been curious about her relationship with Gram.

"I'm not supposed to ask that?" His voice remained soft
and caring.

Teddy wondered if she could even answer. "Right," she
murmured. To her surprise he took her hand and touched her
fingers to his lips, then to hers, and walked off the way he had
come. Teddy could not have been more shocked if he had
really kissed her. Nobody had ever done such a sweet thing
to her before. But then she had never known anyone like
Brandon Sinclair before. Nobody.

The next morning, Teddy stepped back to see how much area the big gun sprinkler was covering. She looked up and noticed the black stallion galloping straight for the dividing fence, with Brand astride, leaning low over the heavily muscled neck. A moment later, Brand dismounted. He stood at the stallion's head, patting him while he yelled at the top of his voice. "Call the dogs. Your pesky goats are all over my place."

"How did they get over there?"

"Walked over the rotten logs you call a fence."

Gram, hearing the ruckus, dropped the wrenches she had been using to set up the irrigation system and ran to Teddy. "Just keep your shirt on, buster. Those llamas won't hurt a thing and we'll have them back in a flash."

"Oh, really? You should have seen my cattle scatter. They won't go near those long-necked camels."

Teddy began laughing. "You don't have to defend me, Gram. Brand has a big mouth, but he won't hurt me. He thinks you're a little mouse defending an elephant . . . me."

"Oh he does, does he? Maybe we should let *him* figure out how to get the llamas off his dumb cattle ranch."

Brand simmered down and grinned. "That mouse and elephant business does sound pretty harsh when you play it back. I'm sorry." He winked. "Now, will you please call your goats home, Gram?"

"I'm not your gram!" she shouted in a voice that would have frightened a tornado cloud. "And they aren't goats. Come on, Teddy, let's go have lunch."

Teddy snatched the old woman's hand and hauled her back beside her. Then she stuck two fingers into her mouth and whistled for the dogs, which appeared almost immediately.

"We better check the fence before you set the dogs on the

llamas," Brand said, leading Thunder northward. "I don't know much about llamas, but cattle can get out of a hole they can't possibly return through."

When they got there, they saw that ten feet of the rotten log fence lay flat on the ground. Teddy instructed the dogs to bring the llamas back, and in a few minutes, the llamas started returning to their own pasture. The dogs did not stop until they had every llama on its own side of the broken-down fence.

"I'll bet those two dogs take the place of a hired man," Brand said. "How would you like to sell them?"

"No way, sonny," Gram said. "We couldn't operate without those dogs." She grinned. "Besides, they don't know what a cow is."

"Okay, I'll have to find my own dogs. How would you girls like to share the expense of putting up wire fencing between our ranches?"

Gram shook her white head. "Not yet. We'll just fix the log fence, even though I'd bet your cattle knocked it down."

Brand's face started to redden. "Wait just a minute, Gram! Were my cattle on your place?"

"No, your cattle are too dumb to walk through the fence they smashed down. And don't you call me Gram!" She turned and walked off. "I'll bring some logs, Teddy," she called.

Brand went home. Teddy finished setting up the irrigation, then joined Gram at the broken-down fence. They spent the afternoon repairing it and went into the house, tired but satisfied with their day's work.

Later in the evening, there was a tap on the front door. "That'll be Lynden," Gram said. They were watching summer reruns on TV; Teddy was working on her red sweater and Gram was cutting out pink butterflies for her quilt.

Lynden settled onto the couch beside Teddy, sprawling until he sat almost on his back. He watched the TV for a few minutes, then looked from Gram to Teddy. "Since you girls aren't watching much, would you mind if I switched to another station?" Without waiting for an answer, he flipped to a program he wanted to watch.

Teddy's eyes met Gram's, who barely raised a bushy, white eyebrow. Teddy's lips turned into a tiny smile. Then she shrugged. "Anything new at work today?" she asked brightly. She always asked because a newspaper should be an exciting place to work.

Lynden shook his head no, held a restraining hand toward her, and leaned closer to the TV.

Gram grinned and Teddy gave her a little push. The big yellow cat climbed into Lynden's lap but he saw nothing except the television.

A few minutes later, Gram laid her scissors down. "Anyone want some pie and ice cream?" she asked.

Teddy pushed her knitting to the back of the needles and dumped it onto the coffee table. "Sure, I'll help."

"Sure nice to have your boyfriend visit a couple of times a week," Gram said with a wicked grin.

"Well, he feels at home," Teddy said. "And I enjoy having him over."

Lynden rushed to wash his hands, accepted the dessert and gulped it, all the while with his eyes glued to the television. "Could just as well have fed him oatmeal," Gram said.

Teddy ate the last bite of her dessert and stood to take the dishes back to the counter when a frenzied attack on the door nearly made her drop the dishes. It actually caused Lynden to look away from the TV.

Teddy threw the door open and Brand strode into the room. Suddenly it felt as though the sun had come from behind a cloud and warmed the entire house.

"Just thought I should check to make sure you girls are all right before I hit the sheets," he said, wearing a wide smile. "I see you aren't."

Gram pointed to Brand's feet. "Take off those boots before you come into my clean house," she yelled.

Brand backed to the front door. "Sorry." He flipped off his boots.

"Now go wash your hands. Those boots are dirty."

Brand complied. "Now, do I get some of whatever you had in those dishes?"

Teddy cut a wide slice of the warm apple pie, piled ice cream beside it, and handed it to him.

"Thanks," he said after he cleaned up the dish. "Hannah's a good cook, but she hasn't produced anything like this." He looked from one to another, then back to Teddy. "Looks as though I interrupted a lively evening."

"What should we have been doing?" Teddy asked.

"Anything. At least you could look more lively."

Gram slapped a long reddish box on the table almost before he finished talking. "Here's a game that'll bring you to life."

"How many are going to play, Gram?" Teddy asked recognizing the box. Gram always hauled it out when they had company because it required four to play.

Everyone looked at Lynden who, eyes on the TV, seemed unaware of anyone's presence. "Looks like it'll be three," Brand said. "What's the game, Gram?"

The little old woman wagged a finger at him. "Nelle," she said, as softly as her gravelly voice could speak. "Pictionary," she said. "Think you could keep up with Teddy and me?"

He raised his golden eyebrows at Gram. "A drawing game?" He smiled at Gram. "If you can do it, so can I. Bring it on."

"We really need four to play this right," Teddy said. "But I just figured out how we can do it with three." She explained that one would draw and the other two guess. The one who drew and the one who correctly guessed would advance their tokens on the board. Brand decided to draw first while Teddy and Gram raced to see who could guess what it was.

"A sailboat?" Teddy yelled.

"No, it's a horse," Gram announced in her gruff voice.

"No!" Teddy bellowed, "it's a table. Those are table legs, Gram."

As the game went on the players grew louder, laughing hysterically as they tried to draw recognizable objects before the sand disappeared from the hourglass.

Finally, Lynden roused himself from the TV and leaned over the papers. "I don't see anything so funny," he said. "Looks stupid to me."

Brand sobered up enough to speak. "Why don't you give it a try, city boy? It may be stupid but it's not easy. And it definitely is funny."

"You three are making major fools of yourselves," Lynden said, dropping into the empty chair. "I'll join you if you play something sensible."

Gram shook her head. "Anybody who *is* anybody is playing this game," she said. "Join us in this one, or go back to your TV."

He watched a little longer, then assuring them he could do much better, agreed to play. He and Teddy became partners and Gram and Brand played together.

When Lynden played, Teddy could not guess what he drew for anything. "It's a marshmallow," she said. "A piece of popcorn. A cotton ball." Lynden soon grew impatient with her. When the time ran out and he told her it was a cloud, she told him clouds are mostly flat on the bottom.

When Gram and Brand crossed the finish line before Teddy and he reached the halfway mark, Lynden jumped up, knocking the playing pieces off the board and onto the table. "I need to go home," he muttered. "I guess I'm the only one here who has to get up at a certain time. I mean with a real job."

Brand bounced to his feet. "What time do you get up, city boy?"

"Seven o'clock . . . no matter what time I get to bed."

Brand shook his head in disbelief. "Is that a fact? Well, I have my cattle all fed by six o'clock. Every morning."

"That's hard for me to believe," Lynden said. "After all, you don't have a boss checking on you. Come on, Teddy, kiss me good night. I have to go." He pulled Teddy to him and covered her mouth with his. She tried to pull back but he held her tightly. Finally, he let her go, put on his shoes, and stepped outside.

Teddy wanted more than anything in the world to go brush her teeth, but Brand stood in the kitchen doorway watching, his eyes mocking her. Unable to control herself, she swiped the back of her hand across her lips. That helped a little, but she knew for sure Brand saw her do it. And that he knew why.

four

"I guess it's time for us all to get to bed," Brand said. "Gram, you're some artist. You just whistle anytime you get the urge to draw again." He laughed softly. "Just be sure we play on the same team again."

"You got that right, sonny. I'm not about to play with that lump of dough that just left."

After Brand had left, Gram turned to Teddy, her faded blue eyes dancing. "You've never been kissed like that before, have you, kitten?"

"No, and I hated it." Teddy shuddered, remembering. "I felt his yucky teeth and. . . . Gram, is something wrong with me?"

"Nope. It's the toad that kissed you. Maybe now you can wake up to find the handsome prince."

"Like who?"

Gram shrugged. "How would I know?"

Teddy took a shower and brushed her teeth. Then she went to bed, wondering what Gram had been babbling about. She had been referring to Brand, of course. After asking God to bless and guide her, she fell asleep.

The next afternoon, Teddy noticed that one of Brand's water gun sprinklers was not rotating. He would have a flood in almost no time if the huge sprinkler was not fixed—it threw out fifty gallons a minute. She dropped the hammer and spit out the nails she had been using to repair a weak spot in the fence between the north and south pastures. Then she dashed to the shed for her wrench and took off toward Brand's place. Thirty minutes later she gave the sprinkler a final testing; she smiled at the smooth and steady way it turned.

Waiting until the hundred-foot stream of water passed the spot where she would climb the fence, she zipped out behind its path and scrambled onto her own property, pleased that she had discovered the problem and helped a neighbor.

She shook her head. She could not be disappointed that Brand had not come out to help. She did not need him. *Why does Brand invade my mind all the time?* Teddy wondered as she continued working on the fence. *I've never spent time dreaming about a man, not even Lynden, and this tall, bronzed giant walks into my life and knocks me completely out of whack.* "Father," she whispered, "I've always been a sensible down-to-earth person. Please help me to stay that way. Thank You." She gathered up her hammer and nails and started working on her fence again.

"I'll bet I can guess whom you aren't thinking about."

Teddy dropped the hammer and nearly swallowed two nails. Brand must be a mind reader. She pressed her hand to her chest. "Okay, whom am I not thinking about?"

"The blob. The one with absolutely no personality."

Teddy stared into his brown eyes . . . the ones where the sunbeams learned how to dance. She said nothing.

"Oh, come on, Teddy, surely you remember the blob. He's the guy who kissed you last night."

"Oh."

"Did you enjoy that kiss?"

Teddy felt her face redden. "What I enjoy and what I don't enjoy couldn't possibly be of interest to you."

"Oh, but it is." He leaned back on his heels and watched

her embarrassment. "When are you going to send him down the road?"

"I have no intentions of sending him down the road. And what makes you think I didn't enjoy the kiss?"

"Because he forced you, kicking and screaming all the way. I was just ready to rearrange his face when he let you go."

He knew. Evidently he stood there with Gram, watching the show they put on. "He's not that bad," she mumbled. "I'm just not into rough kissing, and I thought he wasn't, either. I can't figure out what got into him last night."

"I can. You've heard of animals marking out their territory? Well, that's what that turkey was doing. And I'm still mad about it."

Gram arrived on the scene and heard his remark. "What are you mad about, sonny? Because she's his territory, or that he marked her as his?"

"I don't know, Gram, all of the above? I guess I'm just mad." He pulled his hands from his pockets. "I'd better be getting back. It's about time for evening feeding. See you later." He took off in an easy run and a moment later Teddy and Gram watched him scramble over the old log fence.

"You let him call you 'Gram,' and didn't even yell about it," Teddy said, her bright eyes sparkling.

The leathery old face creased into a wide smile. "I believe I did, at that."

The next Sunday, Lynden took Gram and Teddy to church as usual, and Lynden followed Teddy down the aisle, into the pew. After they sat down, Teddy kept wondering if Brand was in the little church, but she refused to turn around to check. She was in deep thought, enjoying the quiet organ music, when a rustling to her left caused her to meet two laughing brown eyes. Brand scooted through the pew from the other side and sat down beside her.

When the opening hymn was announced, Teddy's hand collided with Brand's as they reached for a hymnal. She pulled back as though his touch was distasteful, but she did not feel that way . . . not even a little bit that way. What was the matter with her, anyway? Then she felt Lynden tense up beside her.

When they rose to sing, Brand motioned for Lynden to share his hymnal with Gram and he held his out for Teddy. Lynden could hardly ignore the sensible-sounding request— there being only two hymnals in each pew—so Teddy shared Brand's book, and learned he had a strong clear baritone voice.

The minister chose for his sermon the verses that said, "Inasmuch as you have done it for the least, you have done it for me." For some reason that made Teddy think of Lynden. She decided she must treat him better. After all he had been coming over for several years and had been faithful and kind all that time. Brand's arrival had upset Lynden as well as her—and she wondered if maybe he had even knocked Gram off her always-even keel.

Afterward, outside in the warm sunlight, Brand held his big brown hand out to Lynden and shook hard. "Great sermon, wasn't it, brother?" Then he turned to Gram. "Hannah has prepared lunch for six, Gram, so could I persuade you folks to help us eat it?"

"Hey, that sounds fantastic," replied Gram. "What do you think, kitten?"

Teddy thought it sounded interesting but she had just told herself to be more considerate to Lynden. She turned to him.

"How about you? Would you rather eat at our place?"

"Frankly, I would, but it looks as if I don't have any choice." His bottom lip puffed out as though a bee had stung it, making him look for all the world like a pouty child. "Are you going to ride with me?" he asked crossly.

"Of course, I'm riding with you," Teddy said. "But you do have a choice, Lynden. I can fix a meal that will fill you up. Really I can. I'd like to go home and change my clothes first anyway. No telling what we'll be doing before the day ends."

After lunch, everyone settled into luxurious white leather chairs and sofas in Brand's comfortable living room and visited for a while.

"Well, my lunch has settled," Brand announced about midafternoon, "how about everyone else's?"

"Yeah," Lynden agreed. "You have a comfortable place here."

"Thanks. Anyone want to go riding?"

Gram was on her feet before he finished talking. "You know, sonny, I thought you'd never ask."

"Me, too. May I ride Misty?" Teddy asked.

"I think I'd better head for home," Lynden said. "Why don't you come on into Bend with me, Teddy? We have plans for later, you know."

She bounced over and captured his hand. "No, you don't. You're going to ride with us. Our plans are for much later."

Brand saddled Powder, a dark fat mare, for Gram. "Just what she needs, Gram, a tiny little lady. She's going to be a mama in about five months."

Then he saddled Misty for Teddy and Pharaoh, the big chestnut gelding for Lynden. "Here's your steed, Greeley, think he'll be fast enough for you?" Brand asked, mischief jumping in his brown eyes.

Lynden looked the gelding up and down, and from one end to the other. "That thing looks pretty big," he mumbled. "And I'm not real used to riding. Maybe you should take him and let me ride yours."

"Okay," Brand agreed. He stepped to the next stall and brought out Thunder. "Here he is. He's the largest stallion in these parts and his name is Thunder for a reason. Do you want to saddle him?"

Lynden looked doubtful as he watched the monstrous horse prance and rear in its eagerness to go. "No, I really think I should be getting back to town."

Gram stepped up to Brand and indicated Lynden with her thumb. "He's pretty skinny. Think he's too heavy for Powder?"

"I suppose not, if he treats her carefully. Did you decide not to ride?"

"No way. I'm riding Pharaoh."

Finally, everyone rode down the long driveway toward the highway. "I know this neat riding trail, about a mile west," Brand said. "Rolf and I've been riding it."

Everyone walked their horses until they hit the trail, then Gram urged Pharaoh into an easy canter. Brand and Teddy followed and Lynden's pregnant mare, Powder, who was not about to be left behind, stepped up to a fast trot. "Hey, Sinclair," Lynden yelled after a few minutes. "How do I stop this thing? It's shaking my teeth out."

"Pull back on the reins, gently," Brand called, but Lynden only heard the first part of the instructions and jerked the reins as hard as he could. At the same time, his heels dug into Powder's tender flanks. The mare stopped short and stood on her hind legs, then put her head down and kicked her back legs straight above her head. Lynden flew several feet into the air, landing on his back on a bed of pine needles.

Teddy sucked in her breath, wondering if Lynden was all right. But Brand instantly flew off his stallion, caught Powder's reins, and examined her mouth. "There, there, girl, we won't let him do it again." He hugged her dark neck and patted her. "I'm sorry, baby, he's just a mean man, but you're all right, now."

Then he turned to Lynden with fury written all over his face. "What were you trying to do?" he bellowed, "Tear her mouth off? Don't you know horses have feelings? Guys like you ruin perfectly good horses."

Lynden struggled to his feet. "If you think I'm climbing back on that horse, you're crazy. You just gave her to me because you knew she'd do something like that."

Brand said something under his breath then stood quietly for a few moments. "If you think I'd let you on any of my horses after that performance," he finally said, "you're the crazy one. Now you just high-tail it back to the ranch. I think there's some candy on the kitchen counter. That ought to keep you busy for a while."

"Gladly. Come with me, Teddy."

Teddy looked at Gram.

"Don't ask me," Gram said. "You already kissed the toad. I don't know what the next act is, but you're going to find out, one way or another."

five

"Please, Teddy," Lynden said quietly. A butterfly's song could have been heard in the ensuing silence. Teddy had been looking so forward to the afternoon ride, but she really should go with Lynden. After all, he had been her boyfriend forever. He wanted her company, and he had a right to ask.

She smiled at the super-thin young man. "Sure, I'll come. What shall I do with Misty, Brand?"

"Uh, bring her to the house and get Rolf. He'll take care of her."

Teddy turned Misty to walk beside Lynden, who now wore a satisfied smile. They had walked a few steps when Brand called to her. "Teddy, would you lead Powder back? You might tell Rolf that Misty feels cheated and needs a nice run. Suggest he come ride with us." He handed Powder's reins to her, mounted Thunder, and turned to Gram. "Okay, Gram, are you ready for some serious riding?"

"Never been more ready in my life. Let's go." Thunder and Pharaoh gracefully galloped away, and Teddy felt morose.

Lynden walked swiftly back toward the highway, with Teddy, riding Misty, beside him, and leading Powder. "Thanks, Teddy, I really wanted a little time alone with you."

"It's all right, I can ride another time. I really do like horses, you know."

"No, I didn't know. Why don't you get some of your own?"

"You know we mortgaged the ranch to the limit when we

42

changed from cattle to llamas. Well, Gram's been putting every spare dime on the mortgage. She took a notion it had to be paid off in five years, and we're right on schedule. Then we can get some horses. And fix up the place. And whatever else—"

"How about I hop up behind you?" Lynden asked, as they turned into Brand's long, long driveway.

Teddy shook her head and slid out of the golden horse's saddle. "I can't, Lynden, but I'll walk with you." Both horses plodded along behind the pair.

"Are you getting hooked on that guy?" Lynden asked.

Teddy shook her head. "He's nice, though," she said quietly.

They talked about inconsequential things until they reached the house, and Lynden went inside for Rolf. He returned a few minutes later with a handful of candy. Teddy laughed out loud. "I see you remembered the candy."

A half-hour later they reached Teddy's house and, after having removed their shoes, they went through the bare living room and flopped onto the kitchen couch. "Well, I guess we got our exercise, even though it didn't turn out quite as I'd planned," Teddy said with a quiet sigh.

Lynden rested a moment, then scrambled to his feet. "I'll make some sandwiches." He opened the refrigerator and pulled out roast beef, mayonnaise, lettuce, and white bread. A short while later, he set the small plate on the coffee table, put two tall glasses of milk beside it, and sat down next to Teddy.

"Aren't you going to ask me if I know anything exciting?" he asked. He took a huge bite of his sandwich, and washed it down with some milk.

"Okay. Hey, Lynden, I was just wondering, have you

learned anything exciting lately?"

He nodded, and wiped his chin with a paper napkin. Then, he pushed himself back on the couch and sat up straight. "It's about your fancy neighbor. Do you still want to hear?"

Suddenly, Teddy did not feel hungry anymore. She laid her sandwich down. "Of course I do. Tell me." She waited a moment, then realized she was holding her breath.

"What do you know about the guy anyway?"

Teddy thought a moment. "Not much." She felt stifled as though the air were too hot to breathe. "Get on with it, Lynden, I'm curious."

"Well, it was this bank robbery in Eugene. Isn't that where he came from? It happened just a few weeks before he showed up here. We got a short item and picture concerning the robbery and it's Sinclair, Teddy. I'd swear it is. Not only the picture and description match, but that truck he drives is the getaway rig."

Teddy shook her head. "No way, not Brand. You have the wrong guy."

"Maybe. Maybe not." He looked so smug that, for a second, she almost did not like him. "How much did that ranch cost, Teddy?"

"I don't know. A bundle, I guess."

He leaned closer to her, his eyes boring into hers. "Where did he get the money? Not too many guys his age have that kind of money and almost as few have the credit to borrow it."

"Where did you see it, Lynden? Show me." Teddy felt breathless, but she would not let Lynden know.

"Well, it hasn't been published in our paper, yet. Since it's old news anyway they'll wait until we have a little space to fill. Who'd ever expect him to be hiding out over here?"

"Could you bring me a copy of the picture? And also the

item? I might even show it to Brand."

Lynden shook his head vigorously. "I'll bring you a copy but you better not show it to Brand. He may be dangerous."

Teddy went to bed that night with Gram's praises of Brand ringing in her ears . . . and his golden good looks floating in her mind, riding like the wind on his beautiful black stallion. *I wish Gram would keep quiet about him,* she told herself, turning over for the ninth time. *He's only a friend. I want to spend my time thinking of Lynden.* But Lynden's face refused to take form in her mind. *What's happening to me? Brand has given me no reason to think about him like this. Besides, he may be a dangerous bank robber.* She laughed out loud at the ludicrousness of that, turned over, and whispered, "Lynden's been my special friend for so long I keep thinking You've given him to me. Is that Your plan for me, Lord? And if Brand's a criminal, won't you help me find out for sure?" Finally, she fell asleep.

Teddy did not see Brand for several days, but her thoughts were constantly on what Lynden had told her. Come to think of it, she did not even know how old Brand was. But he certainly did not look or act like someone hiding from the law. Finally, she could not stand it any longer and asked Gram what she thought.

"Why don't you ask him?" Gram said. "Nothing works as well as communication, I always find."

"I'm not sure why I haven't asked, but Lynden told me not to as he might be dangerous."

"Pish posh," Gram bellowed. "Brand's about as dangerous as Cocoa." Cocoa was one of their best llamas and also one of the gentlest.

Lynden asked Teddy to go to play the following week and

she eagerly looked forward to it. Not only to see the play, which she always enjoyed, but so that she could ask him again about that newspaper article he had mentioned . . . about the Eugene bank robbery. She did not get the chance until they came back at ten-thirty that night after the play.

"Want to come in for a minute?" she asked.

"Sure. For a little while." He sprawled on the couch and pulled the candy dish onto his lap.

She had to ask him now, or she would drive herself crazy wondering. "Anything interesting at the paper these days?"

"No, not in this quiet little town." He unwrapped another mint.

"What about that bank robbery thing? Did it ever get printed?"

He popped the mint between his teeth and reached for another. "I don't think so. I guess the editor thinks there isn't much chance of the guy's being around here. Think I should turn him in?"

"No! I mean, you don't even know if it's him."

He looked sharply at Teddy. "You do have something going with him, don't you?"

"Of course not. You've been with us every time we've tried to do anything. And wrecked it, too, I might add."

Lynden lumbered to his feet. "Well, I'm glad I wrecked your fun with him. I don't approve of his coming around here. Now I have to go home or I'll never get up in the morning."

Teddy walked to the door and waited while he put his shoes on. Then he gave her a peck on the lips, his usual goodbye. "See you Sunday."

The next afternoon Teddy worked on the north pasture

fence again, with the llamas crowding so close she could hardly work. Finally, she threw down her hammer and spent thirty minutes loving her woolly friends.

"Looks like the real thing to me."

Teddy pulled her arm from Romeo's neck and smiled. "What's the real thing?" she asked.

"Love. It looks as if you and your llamas really love each other."

"Oh. Well, we do."

"I suppose you're going to tell me that you know all your llamas by name."

"Of course I do." She started pointing at individual llamas. "That's Lily, there's Cocoa, one of our best young llamas, and there's Angel, Rose is over here, that black one is Belle, Duska is beside Belle . . . and the baby llamas are Peanut, that's the brown one, and—"

Brand cut her off with a deep laugh. "Whoa! We could be at this all day. But one thing I've been wondering about. Have you ever looked across my cattle? All red, wide, and exactly alike?"

Teddy nodded. "Exactly alike."

"Well," Brand continued, "that makes me feel as though my cattle are all the same breed."

"I know. Hereford. That's the kind we raised."

Brand flashed her a friendly smile. "Right. But when I look at your multicolored herd of goats," he shrugged, "I think you have a bunch of mutts."

"You're wrong, Brand. Llamas come in every color from white through reds and browns to blacks, and all mixes. The color doesn't matter and you never know what a female will throw. It's the conformation that counts." She grinned. As Teddy talked, the llamas crowded and bumped them until they could not stand still. "Let's get out of here so we can talk."

In a few minutes, they sat in the lush grass of the empty south pasture about ten feet from the disappointed llamas. As they visited, Teddy could think only about Lynden's terrible news concerning Brand. She just had to find out if it was true. "Uh . . . how old are you?" she asked when a lull developed in the conversation.

"Okay, nosy, I'm almost thirty." He tweaked a dark brown curl. "Old enough to be your father."

"Have you ever been married? Had any kids?"

Teddy thought Brand's eyes opened a bit wider, but he took the question in stride. "I thought I was just getting old enough for those things. Are you applying for the job?"

As Teddy tried to think of a clever answer, something wet and green plopped against his forehead and bounced onto her lap. Brand wiped it off his face while Teddy scraped the horrible stuff from her lap and threw it as far as she could. But that awful odor remained. He took her hand and they ran to the line of old bath tubs that supplied water for the llamas. He washed his face and she literally poured water over her pants. They both washed their hands . . . and washed their hands . . . and washed their hands. When she met Brand's eyes, she realized he was more than unhappy, he was furious!

"I'm sorry," she began, "I didn't see Casanova around this morning. He must have come up after we left the llamas."

He started off toward his own ranch, muttering under his breath. The rest of the day seemed colder and darker to Teddy. In fact, she barely noticed when the sun dropped behind the trees. When she could not see to drive nails anymore, she quit and trudged to the house.

Gram offered no sympathy when told about the incident. "Don't worry, kitten, he'll get over it."

But Teddy did worry. She had a hard time getting to sleep, thinking about Brand. He might not come back anymore, after two run-ins with Casanova. Then her mind wandered to the news that Lynden had so eagerly pressed into her ear. If Brand had any criminal tendencies he was the best actor she had ever met. Well, what was it to her, anyway?

The next morning Teddy filled the watering tubs and checked through the llamas, especially the young ones, making sure everybody was happy and well. As she worked, she thought of Brand. She had to admit she hoped he did get over being mad. He really did brighten her days. After she finished feeding, she remembered she had not noticed Casanova. She walked back through all the milling llamas and still did not see him.

six

Oh well, how could she expect to see each of 500 llamas every time? Still, it bothered her and she mentioned it to Gram at breakfast.

"Let's go have another look," Gram said.

They wandered through the herd for an hour and a half but did not spot the large red and white llama. "We can look again after lunch, Gram. He's probably lying down somewhere in the shade."

But several more checks convinced Teddy that Casanova had disappeared. Where could he have gone? No llama had ever disappeared before. Not only was Casanova a good friend, but they had paid $14,000 for him. And for Romeo, too. They were top breeding stock. A ranch the size of Teddy's—one of the largest in the United States—must breed good stock.

That night, Gram busily cut out pieces for her quilt and Teddy worked on her red sweater. She hoped to finish it that evening and start on the matching skirt. "Just how mad was your neighbor when he left the other day?" Gram asked.

Teddy laughed. "Pretty mad, and I don't blame him. You can't believe how awful that stuff is."

"Mad enough to do something to Casanova?"

Teddy's throat constricted and a fat lump formed too far down to swallow. No. Brand would not do something to any animal. He was too kind. But where could the big llama have gone? After asking her Heavenly Father to care for the llama, Teddy felt better and went to bed.

The next morning, Gram went with Teddy to do the morning chores, and they both searched behind every tree and in all the sheds, as well as among the many sizes and colors of llamas. He simply was not on the place.

"I think we owe our neighbor a visit," Gram said, after they finished washing the breakfast dishes.

"Maybe just one of us should go, Gram. He might think we're being unfriendly if we both go."

"He might be right, too," Gram said, nodding her head.

They both took off across the uninhabited south pasture. After climbing the old log fence, they trotted across Brand's pasture, through his yard, and up to the house. Gram banged on the front door; Teddy wished she were small enough to hide behind the tiny old lady.

Brand's middle-aged helper, Hannah, opened the door. "Well, our neighbors. I've been wishin' you'd come see me." She opened the door wide. "Come right in. I'll fix something to munch on."

Teddy stepped forward and ran into Gram's steel arm. "We didn't come for socializing," Gram said in a stern voice. "We'd like to see Mr. Sinclair."

"He ain't here, Mrs. Marland. He and Rolf had a business engagement in Sisters this morning. Think they hauled an animal over there. I don't know when they'll be back."

"Humph! You tell Mr. Sinclair we have urgent business with him the minute he gets back. Understand?"

Hannah nodded. "I understand, Mrs. Marland. I hope everything's all right."

"Just tell him." Gram turned Teddy around and marched her down the steps.

Neither said a word until they jumped the fence into their own property. Then Teddy stopped Gram and looked into her faded blue eyes. "You don't think they hauled Casanova to the Patterson Ranch do you?" The Patterson Llama Ranch was *the* largest in the country and located in the tiny town of Sisters.

"I'd rather think that than that he killed the animal."

"It could have been someone else, Gram."

"Sure, and Brand wasn't mad at Casanova."

"Someone could have taken him for the money."

"Come on, kitten, your brain's turning to mush," Gram puffed as they trotted across their pasture. "Anyone who knows how much Casanova's worth would know Cocoa and several other females are worth twice that much or more. Don't you think they'd be likely to rustle the females—or both?"

Teddy's mind felt like mush all right. She had had enough worries, fearing some of the llamas might get sick and die after mortgaging the ranch to pay for them, now she had to start worrying about rustling.

An hour later, Brand drove his black truck down the driveway amid a cloud of dust, turned into the yard and skidded thirty feet to a stop. He ran to the front porch, where Gram and Teddy sat, taking a breather from their work.

"Hannah said you girls are all upset about something," he said. Breathing hard, he plopped down on the front steps. "How can I help?"

"What did you go to Sisters for?" Gram asked in a voice resembling a moose's call.

Brand's eyebrows shot up in surprise. "We sold an un-needed animal," he answered a moment later. Another long silence followed. "Have I done something wrong?" he finally asked. He looked from Gram to Teddy and back to Gram.

Teddy could not answer. In fact, she could not bear to be making this rift. But Gram did not seem to mind. "Any idea how much a good breeding llama's worth?" she asked.

After a short silence that seemed an eternity, Brand answered. "No, Gram, I don't. I hadn't considered it vital information to my operation."

"Well, it's vital to our operation, young man. We paid $14,000 for that llama that spits."

Brand whistled. But his eyes never left Gram's face. Then he shook his golden head. "Seems like an animal worth that much money could learn who his friends are, doesn't it?"

Gram jumped from her chair and towered over Brand, who still sat on the top step. "I've had enough game playing, Brand. Why don't you just tell us what you've done with Casanova."

Brand sprang up beside Gram, reversing positions, and peered down at her, the benign expression gone from his face. "What do you think I've done with that cheap camel? I haven't been near him—and believe me that's the way it's going to stay." His stormy gaze met Gram's thunderous one. "I hate that animal!" he finished, with feeling.

Gram nodded. "So you hate him. I'll ask you once more. What did you do with him?"

In the moment that followed, Brand's eyes lighted with understanding. "Oh, you mean you want to know what I did *to* him, do you? Well, I shot him and fed him to my cattle." He cast one furious look at Teddy and stomped down the steps.

"Well, what do you think?" Gram asked, as they watched the truck disappear in a cloud of angry dust.

"I think he's innocent."

"I don't know. He got pretty riled."

"Wouldn't you? If someone accused you of purposely doing someone out of $14,000?"

As Teddy went about her work that afternoon she thought about Brand. If he did do something to Casanova, then he probably robbed the bank too. She did not exactly know why one would have anything to do with the other, but that is how she felt.

The next Sunday, Brand did not sit beside Teddy at church, and she felt very lonely. Even though she felt she had lost a personal friend in Casanova, and that they could hardly handle a financial loss of that magnitude, the fact that Brand would do such a thing was the most painful thought to Teddy. She had been so sure that he would not even step on an ant. Later at home, Lynden seemed unusually happy. "I wonder why the big cowboy didn't push himself on us today."

"Because one of our llamas spit on him," Gram said in a hard voice.

Lynden burst into one of his rare fits of laughter. He slapped his knee. "Fantastic! How did you get her to do it?"

"It was Casanova," Teddy explained. "And this was the second time he did it. Somehow he took a dislike to Brand."

"Wise animal."

A lot you know, Teddy thought. *You have never shown the slightest interest in our llama herd.*

"Lunch is ready. Have you washed your hands?" Gram asked, looking sharply at Lynden.

He held out his hands. "As soon as I came in, Nelle," he answered with a good-natured laugh. "You have me trained."

Teddy put the roast on the table and slipped into her chair. Lynden speared a piece of meat almost before Gram finished asking the blessing. "The thing is," Gram said, "Casanova has disappeared now. Completely gone." She helped herself to a large roasted potato and drowned it with brown gravy.

Lynden took two more bites of roast beef, then his eyes snapped to Gram's. "Did you say Sinclair did something violent to your llama?"

Gram's eyes never left her plate, but she nodded slowly. "I think I'd say that."

Lynden dropped his fork onto his plate, forgetting his food for the moment. "This just might be the story that'll get me the advancement I deserve. After we finish eating, I'll write it up."

"No you won't." Teddy laid her own fork on the edge of her plate. "We have no idea what happened to Casanova, other than he's gone."

Lynden laid an assuring hand on Teddy's arm. "I'll just write a story about the disappearance of a valuable animal. Then I'll casually mention that it spit on Sinclair the day before it disappeared." He burst into laughter again. "I'll bet he was really mad."

Teddy nodded. "I don't blame him a bit. I got it, too, and it's awful stuff."

After lunch, the three sat around visiting. About an hour later, Gram became restless. "Did you notice I mowed the lawn?" she asked.

"I did, Gram. It looks beautiful and smells heavenly." She grinned at her wiry grandmother. "We really should mow more than three times a year. I mean I should, not you."

"Right. Well, I mowed it so we could play croquet this afternoon. If we don't watch out, summer will be gone with no croquet games."

In a little while the wickets all stood in their proper spots and the players had each chosen a mallet. Gram made each play count, but Teddy and Lynden could not seem to get going. They were still headed toward the far post when a black pickup truck drove slowly up the driveway. It stopped near the house and a short balding man jumped out.

"Would you happen to be missing a llama?" he called.

Everyone dropped their mallets, the game forgotten. "We sure are," Teddy said. "It's a red and white male. A really huge one."

The man nodded. "That's him. You pay for the damage he's done and he's yours. Personally, I wouldn't have the filthy thing. He crawled over the fence and bred my two females. Then he spat on me when I tried to catch him." The man looked at each of them to determine the effect his story had. "And I wanted my females bred to something really good," he finished sadly.

"Well, don't shed too many tears about that, junior," Gram said to the middle-aged man. "You got a lot more than you bargained for. That llama's worth a mint, and his breeding services go for $3000, but since he called on you, uninvited, I guess you just received a $6,000 gift."

The man's face brightened. "Are you sure? He's really worth all that much?"

Lynden nodded emphatically, as though he knew all about llamas.

"I'll follow you home and collect him right now," Teddy said.

When Casanova saw Teddy he ran toward her as though he would smash her into the ground. But Teddy held out her arms to the big llama, who skidded to a stop beside her. Then he nuzzled her face, obviously happy to see her. "Come on, you big turkey, let's go," she said, walking toward the open gate with her arm over Casanova's back. She steered him to the horse trailer and he walked in.

"Well, Brand didn't do Casanova in," Teddy said to Gram that evening. "I guess we owe him another visit."

"Yep. Fair is fair," said Gram. "Let's get going."

Brand's eyes opened with surprise when he answered his doorbell. He did not smile, but looked at Gram warily. "Good evening," he said, without expression.

Gram put her tiny wrinkled hand on Brand's arm. "May we come in, sonny?" she asked kindly. "We have something to say."

Brand backed up. "I thought you said it all the last time." He hesitated a moment, then swung the door wide open. "Sure. Come in."

"We wanted you to know that Casanova's safe and sound," Gram began.

"Oh, so I'm exonerated. I'm sure glad he turned up. Otherwise I'd have been guilty forever, wouldn't I?"

"Teddy knew you didn't do it, Brand."

Brand offered Teddy a small smile. "Thanks."

"Well, young man, would you like to know what happened to Casanova?"

"I'm sure you're going to tell me."

"He heard the song of romance and deserted his many wives for a new love," Gram said, obviously trying to make Brand laugh.

Brand nodded. "I figured as much. You really need to get a fence together that will keep your camels inside."

After a little while of forced conversation, Gram told Teddy they should go home.

Teddy got up then turned to Brand. "We came to say we're very sorry we accused you of doing something to him. I know you're much too kind to do something like that."

Brand almost smiled. "Oh, I'm not so sure about that. But

I'm way too scared of that spitting fool to try anything with him. As far as I'm concerned, his weapon is deadly."

Back home, Teddy and Gram started work on their respective projects. "What did you think, Gram?" Teddy asked.

"I think he's a nice boy. Why do you ask?"

"Do you think he'll be able to forgive us?"

"Of course he will. Just give him a little time."

"Do you think this means he's not the guy that robbed the bank?"

Gram threw back her head and laughed. "I don't see what one has to do with the other, but didn't you ask him?"

"Not exactly. I asked him some personal questions and somehow never got around to that one. He ended up thinking I was proposing to him."

Gram thought that one over for a minute. "He's not the kind of person who'd do something dishonest. I doubt he'd even cheat on his income tax and that's borderline." Teddy did not laugh. The sound of Gram's scissors carefully cutting out several butterfly parts snipped a duet with Teddy's clicking needles for a few minutes. Then, Gram laid the scissors down. "I was kidding about income tax, you know. Cheating's never borderline. To God, cheating's stealing. And we know the commandments." They worked in silence for a while. "Now, maybe I'll get to ride Pharaoh again," Gram said. "I'd been worrying about that."

Teddy laughed. "Shame, Gram. I never thought you'd be so small."

"Oh, pshaw. You've always known I wasn't very big."

Teddy hugged Gram and trudged off to bed. Tomorrow would be another busy day, just like all the rest. She asked God to watch over her, keep her on the right track, and fell asleep in the middle of the *Amen*.

All the next day, Teddy watched over her shoulder, hoping to see a big golden man striding toward her, but Brand did not show up. Nor the next day or the next.

When Teddy walked into church beside Lynden the following Sunday, her mind was not on the man she came with. Would Brand come and sit beside her? Just having his big frame beside her on the pew would make her happiness complete for that one day. Her heart beat loudly as she peeked fearfully back toward the door.

seven

Teddy quickly determined the big man was not in the church. She was not brave enough to turn around again, but her senses stayed tuned to the back. "*Forgive me, God,*" she silently prayed when she discovered she had missed the entire service waiting for Brand.

After the benediction, Gram led her little group outside into the sunshine where the members greeted each other and visited briefly. Then, Teddy saw Brand getting into his sports car, and he was not alone! A tall, dark-haired girl sat in the passenger seat, looking very happy.

"Do I detect a grump in you today?" Lynden asked after Teddy had cleared the lunch dishes away and joined him on the couch. "It couldn't have anything to do with that fox Sinclair had with him, could it?"

"Why should I care who he has with him?" Teddy asked testily.

"Well, I care who Brand had with him," Gram said. "I was hoping to go riding this afternoon. That Pharaoh's some animal. I can't handle an afternoon of doing nothing. Maybe I'll ride a llama."

A big laugh burst from Teddy and she felt better. "Maybe we'll all ride llamas," she said, joining Gram's foolishness.

Teddy and Gram spent the following days fertilizing and watering the alfalfa field. They also kept busy with their other duties, such as irrigating the pastures and caring for the llamas. They always had fencing that needed repairing, but it had to wait its turn. Teddy kept an eye out for Brand all week, but he seemed to be busy elsewhere.

Friday night, Lynden took Teddy to a movie in Bend starring Kurt Russell. "I suppose you think that Russell guy is some kind of sex symbol," Lynden kidded while they drank milk shakes later.

Teddy nodded. "As a matter of fact, he's gorgeous. Admit it, Lynden."

Lynden laughed. "He isn't to me. You are, though." Looking a little surprised at his own words, he took the straw back into his mouth and noisily sucked his half-melted drink.

Teddy felt her face redden. She had been thinking she was just another friend to him and here he gives her a compliment. The very first one! Ever!

"Thanks, Lynden." She pushed the large, frost-covered glass to one side and leaned on her elbows. "That was a sweet thing to say. You're so nice to keep taking me around and I truly appreciate it. You're a good friend, and I enjoy being with you. But is that enough? Shouldn't you be looking for someone who will fall gloriously, crazily in love with you?"

Lynden snapped to attention. His eyes narrowed and his lips straightened into a hard line. "Is that how you feel about Sinclair?"

"Of course not. I'm not ready for a serious relationship. That's why I wanted to talk with you."

"Are you sure?"

"Of course I'm sure. I've barely seen Brand when you weren't with us."

Lynden released an audible sigh. "I'll take your word for it then. I guess we may as well carry on as we have been. I enjoy your company, too, and I'm also not ready to get

serious with anyone." He chuckled. "Not rich enough,
anyway. But our friendship means everything to me. I vote
we carry on." He reached his right hand across the restaurant
table and shook hers firmly.

A wide smile lighted Teddy's face. "Okay. Great. But I
have one addition to our relationship. We'll take turns
paying from now on, okay?"

He shook his head. "We both know what a bum I am,
hanging around your place all the time, eating off you.
You're lucky if it equals out. And I do enjoy both you and
your grandmother."

Teddy went to bed that night wondering exactly what had
happened in that restaurant. She had intended to cool things
with Lynden a little, and now she liked him better than she
ever had. He had shown insight and sensitivity she had not
known he possessed. But she still liked him only as a good
friend.

Brand smiled and greeted Teddy and Gram at church that
Sunday but did not introduce them to the dark-haired girl
who was very much with him.

Back home, Teddy tried desperately to hide the depres-
sion she felt. Surely Brand's girlfriend had nothing to do
with her feelings, even though she could still see the girl
laughing into Brand's eyes while he looked as though he
would like to kiss her. The girl's black hair and eyes looked
at least part Spanish. With her olive skin and highly-colored
cheeks and lips, Teddy had never seen a more beautiful
woman in her entire life. Not that she minded Brand having a
beautiful woman—he deserved it as much as anyone else. And
their contrasting looks, his bright hair and her dark, comple-
mented each other. She was glad for him . . . well, she was.

Lynden and Gram appeared not to notice Teddy's funk and the day finally disappeared into a hazy oblivion.

Tuesday morning, Teddy opened her water gate at six o'clock and started getting the irrigation set up so she could use every drop of water that ran into her pond that day.

"What're you going to do when you finish that?"

Teddy's heart doubled in size instantly and she could barely breathe. She had not talked to Brand for two weeks and here he was, right beside her, in gorgeous living color.

"This will take a while. Did you need something?" Teddy hoped he could not detect her breathlessness. Or, if he did, maybe he would think it was from moving the long pipe.

"I don't need anything, but you do. I'm pretty well caught up right now and I wondered if you'd like some help. We could try to make those rickety fences last another year or two."

"Thanks, Brand. Gram and I will be working on fences as soon as I finish here, but I can't think of any reason you should help."

His wide lips parted in a smile. "To protect the neighborhood? And my good name? How about to keep a nice old lady off the streets—I mean pastures?"

Teddy nodded. An afternoon off would not hurt Gram a bit. She probably took the old woman too much for granted. "Sure, that would be nice. I'll be ready to start early this afternoon."

He took the big wrench from her hands. "I'll help you with this job, which incidentally is much too heavy for a woman, and we'll get on the fence in a couple of hours."

They hooked up several water gun sprinklers and tested them. They all worked fine, except a new one that refused to turn. Teddy worked on the sprinkler head while Brand walked on down the line to check a connection. After she forced a few drops of oil into the right place, the sprinkler began its slow circular motion, shooting a large stream of water more than a hundred feet. She watched it move smoothly in its circle a moment, then, acting on an impulse, spun the head until it drenched Brand.

"Hey!" He lowered his head and charged toward Teddy, but not until the water had soaked him through. Teddy laughed wildly when he reached her dry spot.

Brand shook his head, sending droplets over Teddy. "You did that on purpose, didn't you?" he yelled. Grasping her by her arm, he took off running—right into the heavy deluge.

Teddy gasped. That water was colder than she had expected. She tried to jerk free, but Brand held tightly, laughing down at her, his dripping hair hanging in points over his forehead. In less than a minute she was as wet as he. They laughed and shouted like two children, pushing each other into the spray as it came around, and playfully trying to escape from the other's grasp. Finally, they ran from the water into the warm sunlight and stood looking at each other for a long moment.

Brand broke the spell. "Recess is over, kid. Hit the trail." They worked as energetically together as they had played, neither saying much.

By mid-morning they finished the irrigation and started on the much easier fence repairing. Brand lifted the heavy logs and Teddy drove the huge nails.

"Did you know you have a pretty cute grandmother?" Brand asked, sometime later.

Teddy nodded and pulled a nail from her mouth. "Only the greatest. And she can work as long and hard as I." She shoved the nail back between her teeth and swung the four-pound hammer with all her strength.

They worked a couple of hours without talking, then Brand took the hammer from her and pulled her to the ground beside him. "Break time," he said.

Teddy gladly relaxed, allowing the warm sun to continue drying her soaked clothing and hair. "Gram and I don't know the meaning of breaks," she said, searching for something to say. "We work until we finish and quit."

Brand studied Teddy as though he wanted to say something, but remained quiet.

Gram seemed to be a good subject, Teddy decided. "Gram sure enjoyed riding Pharaoh."

Brand nodded. "I know. She should ride again. And you, too. You haven't even had one good ride, yet. That, uh, blob that hangs around won't let you finish."

Teddy decided to ignore the slur Brand had aimed at Lynden. "Gram really wanted to ride Sunday, but I wouldn't let her interrupt you with your new friend."

"You mean Celia? You tell Gram she can come over and ride anytime she wants. Celia would be glad to have her join us."

So ... Celia did ride with Brand. Teddy felt like crying but she took a deep breath and swallowed. "Does Celia ride Misty?" she murmured without looking up.

"No, she rides her own horse. That's where we met, on that trail I tried to take you on." Brand put his finger under Teddy's chin and lifted it until her eyes met his. "Don't you want her riding Misty?" he asked softly.

Teddy's eyes dropped to her lap. She swallowed again. For some reason it really hurt her to imagine anyone else on Misty, especially Celia. Or could it be that she did not want anyone else with Brand? "She's your horse," she replied. "I don't care who rides her."

Brand hopped lightly to his feet and held his hand to help Teddy. "Break's over," he said, handing Teddy her large hammer.

They had not worked long when Gram roared up on her motor bike. "I fixed lunch for you two," she yelled over the motor. "Figured it was the least I could do since I'm having the day off." She gave it the gas and roared away across the pasture.

Teddy dropped her hammer and followed Brand toward the old ranch house.

Several hours, much friendly conversation, and many feet of repaired fence later, Brand and Teddy rested on the pasture floor again. He looked as though he wanted to say something, just as he had earlier in the day.

"Say it," Teddy said, laughing. "You're bursting with something, so spit it out before we both shatter into fragments."

Brand hesitated, then shook his head. "No, I better not." Then he smiled. "Maybe I'll ask this instead. How are things going between you and the boy reporter?"

"Just fine. He's trying hard to get a promotion."

A scowl drew Brand's golden eyebrows almost together. A moment later he got to his feet. "I think I'd better call it a day," he said. "I still have several things to do before Celia comes over to ride."

Teddy scrambled to her feet, too. "Okay, thanks a lot for the help. We repaired as much fence in one day as Gram and I would have in three."

They separated, Teddy walking toward her house and Brand heading for the fence that divided their two places. "I notice I didn't get an invite to ride with the beautiful Celia and Brand," she muttered to herself as she crossed the pasture.

Teddy did not eat much supper that night; she was not hungry. After supper, Gram kept looking at her as they watched TV and worked on their projects. "Are you sick, kitten?" she asked.

Teddy grinned. "Almost. Gram, do you think I could be in love with Brand Sinclair?"

Gram's blue eyes glistened. "I don't see you how you could *not* be in love with him. I know I am."

"Come on, Gram. I mean really."

"So do I. Now, what are you going to do about it?"

"I don't know. Once upon a time he acted as if he knew I was a woman. But he never notices anymore."

eight

Brand arrived early the next morning to put in another day repairing fences, so Teddy chased Gram inside again. "Just to the house, Gram, not to a home," she said, patting Gram on her curly top.

"What was that all about?" Brand asked after Gram left.

"She's feeling somewhat useless. But a little rest won't hurt her a bit."

They worked well together and the fence began to look as though it would hold for several more years. After a long comfortable silence, Teddy began to search for a topic of conversation. "How was your ride yesterday afternoon?" she asked, then wished she had not brought up the subject.

He leaned back on his heels. "Great," he said. "We had a long, relaxing ride."

Teddy held a nail to the log and smashed it into the old wood with a vengeance. She just bet they had had a long, relaxing ride. But she had to ask . . . and she really did not want to know one thing about those two. Well, what she really wanted was for there to be nothing between them for her to know.

"Did city boy come over and eat all your candy last night?" Brand asked.

Teddy straightened up and returned Brand's wicked grin. "No, he comes only on Tuesdays and Fridays . . . just like my water."

"And just as welcome I suppose."

Teddy made a big deal out of hesitating before answering.

"Uh, well, maybe just a teeny bit more so, I guess."

Gram made lunch for Brand and Teddy again and they worked until five o'clock. He laid the last log over and held it for Teddy to nail, then wiped his hands on his jeans. "Guess that about does it for today," he said.

"Why, do you have to go riding again?" Now why did she do that? The last thing she wanted to know was what those two did every night.

He scowled, as though trying to figure her out. "I hadn't planned to, but would you and Gram like to go after supper? According to the schedule, your paper boy wouldn't interfere tonight."

Teddy felt as tired as she ever had in her entire life, and her arm ached from swinging that hammer. Keeping up with Brand took everything she had and a little more. *Father, help me get rested up really quickly tonight, okay? Thanks.* "I wasn't fishing for an invitation, but I'll check with Gram. I didn't realize how much she likes to ride."

His smile outshone the sun. "Great. I'll be waiting to hear."

Gram could not wait to ride, so Teddy called Brand and accepted his invitation while Gram put supper on the table. Both women wolfed down the food in anticipation of the planned activities. Then Teddy noticed that she felt a lot better. Almost no aches or pains from swinging the heavy hammer and well rested. *Thanks, God,* she tossed silently into the sky.

Brand had the three horses saddled and ready to go when Gram and Teddy arrived. Powder, the dark mare, reached her head over the fence to Teddy, who petted her and talked to her a few minutes.

"I'll say thanks for Powder," Brand said. "She doesn't get

as much attention as she'd like, now that we seldom ride her."

Gram rode Pharaoh, Teddy the dainty palomino, Misty, and Brand climbed on Thunder, the huge black stallion. They rode on the trail for two hours and returned well exercised and feeling better, including the horses. But Brand treated Teddy as a good friend. Period.

He helped repair fences all week, except when he handled his own irrigation, but did not cast a look or say a word to indicate he thought any more of her than a neighbor who needed a hand.

Lynden took Teddy and Gram to church again, and Brand took Celia. Although Brand's greeting could not have been more cordial, he did not stop to visit and therefore did not introduce Celia.

After eating the delicious meal Teddy and Gram had prepared and emptying the candy bowl, Lyndon invited Teddy to sit with him on the couch. "I brought that article," he said, "as well as another that just arrived in the office." He pulled an envelope from his jacket pocket.

Teddy, sitting beside him, instructed herself to breathe calmly as he pulled the bits of paper from the envelope and placed them in her hand. She unfolded the picture first that turned out to be from the hidden camera in the bank. The picture of the man holding the gun was so fuzzy no one could identify anyone from it, but, it showed he had blond hair, wide shoulders, lean hips, and long, long legs. She drew in a long breath and handed it back to Lynden. "I see the resemblance, but lots of men look like that. You could never, ever use that picture to identify Brand."

She unfolded the two articles and read them, learning little. "I don't think you could identify Brand from these articles either," she said. "All I see that could help is that the man has a guttural voice—and Brand's voice is anything but guttural."

Lynden put the articles and picture back into the envelope. "Well, people do strange things with their voices, you know. And it gives a pretty good physical description of the man, Teddy. Did you read it? It matches Sinclair closer than you could describe me."

Teddy had to agree but managed to get the subject changed for the entire afternoon.

Gram and Teddy had a talk that evening after Lynden finally left. "I'm afraid I must give you that advice I spoke of," Gram said. "You're going to have to get rid of Lynden." Gram sat at the table, tracing the butterfly pattern onto pink broadcloth. "That is if you want Brand to notice you. He's an honorable man and right now he sees you as Lynden's girlfriend."

Teddy had been thinking along the same lines. "I don't know if I can, Gram. Lynden's really nice. And he hasn't done anything to deserve being dumped. I guess I feel sorry for him."

"Feeling sorry for someone in a situation like this is like taking a week to drill a root canal. Believe me, it'll be less painful if you do it quickly and get it over with."

Teddy remembered Lynden's articles about someone like Brand being sought for that dumb bank robbery. "I have another reason to stay in touch with Lynden, Gram. Remember him saying that Brand robbed a bank just before he came here?"

Gram shoved out a hand, as though pushing the thought away. "Posh. Don't believe everything you hear. Brand didn't do anything of the sort."

"I know he didn't do it, but I still want to learn everything I can about it. I'll have a talk with Lynden, Gram, that I'd like to remain friends with him if he'll do that."

Gram nodded wisely. "All right. Then you and Lynden will understand how it is, but how's Brand going to know?"

Teddy thought about that after she went to bed that night. As far as Brand would know, she and Lynden would still be romantically involved. But she could not walk up to the man and explain that she was now available, could she? And did she have any slight fears that Brand might be the bank robber? No, he could never do something like that. Even so, she doubted she could be cruel enough to completely follow Gram's suggestion of totally dumping Lynden.

A couple of days later, in the afternoon, Gram and Teddy started clipping the llamas' toenails, a job they dreaded but did anyway every three months. Llamas have split hooves like cattle, but a small nail that grows out over the hoof has to be clipped, somewhat like a human toenail. By evening they had finished about sixty llamas, and, after the usual feeding and watering, both women were more than ready to quit for the day.

They started again the next morning right after six o'clock and were going fine when Thunder, with Brand aboard, galloped up the driveway and back to the barn where they worked.

Brand dismounted and approached the women. "Looks as though you two are keeping out of mischief today." He watched a moment. "Hey, I never have to clip my cattle's hooves. Are you sure you wouldn't like to go back to raising cattle?"

Gram's blue eyes flashed. "Not on your life, sonny.

Llamas are more human to handle, if you get my drift. You can have the cattle."

Brand pulled off his Stetson and shoved his hair back. "That's sort of what I'm here for. I'm loading 200 head of cattle today. We have the near ones in the corral, but over 100 have escaped to the back of the pasture. We're having a terrible time. I was wondering, do you think your dogs would run cattle?"

Gram jerked her head toward Teddy. "You go help. I'll carry on here."

Teddy finished her llama, released it, then stood up and stretched. "These dogs have never even seen cattle, as far as I know, let alone worked them, but we'll see what happens."

Brand put Teddy on the horse with him and the dogs ran alongside. Thunder took them out to the pasture where the ill-mannered cattle milled around, bawling nervously. Teddy called the dogs and told them to take the cattle in. They cocked their heads and she motioned at the cattle. When they understood what she wanted, they went to work, quietly but effectively. Soon, the cattle bunched together, moving slowly toward the gleaming white corrals, where several huge trucks awaited their turns at the loading chutes.

"Well, looks as if everything's under control," Teddy said, her nostrils filled with the stench of many cattle.

"Yeah," Brand answered, never taking his eyes off the two dogs working together. "Those dogs are worth their weight in gold. Didn't we say they took the place of a man? Well that bunch of steers ran through six men, and the two dogs are handling them just fine."

Teddy nodded, satisfied. "I'm glad. I didn't know whether they'd work cattle, but they're great dogs." She had one more comment she wanted desperately to make but hardly dared. She drew in a deep breath. "I hated to be a party to what you're doing to those cattle," she said. "Can you blame them for running off? They were only trying to save their lives."

Brand nodded. "I thought of that. I feel sorry for them, and no, I don't blame them. This earth isn't perfect, is it? Did you know the Bible tells us that after Jesus returns to claim His own nothing will be hurt or destroyed anymore?"

The dogs driving the cattle into the corrals where they would be loaded into the trucks interrupted the conversation. Brand sent several quick glances Teddy's way as they walked slowly along.

Sensing him watching her, Teddy began to feel embarrassed. Then she stumbled and nearly stepped in a fresh pile of manure. "Your pasture's a mess," she told Brand, laughing. "I'd forgotten how filthy cows are. Sure you don't want to change to llamas?"

"Don't tempt me. Seriously, I couldn't afford to right now, no matter how badly I wished. I invested all my ready money in the cattle."

All the money you got in the bank heist? No! She knew better than that. How could she even let a thought like that pass through her head?

Another silence fell between them. Teddy felt Brand struggling with himself again. "I owe you one," he finally said. "How can I repay you?"

"How about a steak dinner for the dogs?"

He shook his head. "How about a steak dinner for you?"

"You don't owe me; I didn't do a thing."

He reached for her hand and held it until they stepped up to the corral. Then, after slipping the board that locked in the recalcitrant animals, he turned back to Teddy. "I'm afraid I'd feel embarrassed, taking two dogs out to dinner. Won't you go? Please?"

What about Celia, Teddy wondered. But she could think of nothing in the whole world she would like better than to go with Brand . . . anywhere, anytime. So why not?

"If you'd be more comfortable, and your cub reporter would feel better, Gram could come, too," Brand offered just as Teddy opened her mouth to accept his invitation.

"All right, we accept. She'll do justice to any steak you can buy."

Brand's eyes shone as though the sun lived in his head rather than in the cloudless, blue sky above. "Great. How about Saturday night? Let's dress up, okay?"

Thunder, Misty, and Brand took Teddy back home. Brand delivered Teddy to her door, saluted smartly and trotted off down the driveway leading Misty. She hurried inside to tell Gram about Brand's taking them out to dinner. Finding an empty house, she hurried out to the barn where Gram still trimmed toenails.

"It worked, Gram. Brutus and Caesar did just great. And Brand's taking us out to dinner Saturday night. For a sort of reward, I guess. I tried to get him to take the dogs, but he thought he'd be embarrassed."

Gram sat on a small wooden box, working on a quiet llama's toenail. Her furrowed face wrinkled into a big smile. "That's fine. Just fine, but I'm not going." Her rough voice sounded happy. "Stand still, Daisy, I'm not hurting you. Dating's for young people, not an old, worn-out woman. Besides, I heard somewhere that three's a crowd."

Teddy picked up her trimmers and started on Maybe, a gray and white llama with an all-gray, female baby llama by her side. "But you have to go this time, Gram. He expressly invited you. If he wants to take me out alone, he'll ask."

By Saturday night, Teddy and Gram finished trimming
the llamas' nails and felt like celebrating the finishing of the
big job. "Brand said we were supposed to dress up," Teddy
said as Gram came from the bathroom, her curls even tighter
than usual, and smelling of powder and cologne.

"Oh, he did, did he? Okay, it doesn't matter to me." The
old lady flashed a toothy smile and disappeared into her
bedroom. Teddy gratefully took her turn in the shower,
hoping to wash her internal butterflies down the drain.

After she dried her dark hair with a blow dryer, she used
a curling brush to make it perfect for the evening. She chose
a long dress of huckleberry-colored satin and taffeta. The
double-puffed sleeves accentuated the simple waist and the
double ruffle at the bottom of the outer skirt turned up in the
back and narrowed to a V at the waist, creating a bustle
effect. After arranging the dress to her satisfaction, Teddy
deftly applied makeup, something she hardly ever bothered
with. Tonight she wanted Brand to notice her.

She stepped into the living room to find Gram already
there, her head twisted around, checking her jeans for
something. "Do you see something on the back of my
pants?" she asked. "Cat hair, maybe?"

Teddy brushed the back of the already clean jeans.
"They're fine, Gram."

Gram looked Teddy over, from shining hair to matching
huckleberry sandals. "You really like the guy, don't you,
kitten? Think he'll notice you?"

"Did I overdo it, Gram?"

"No way. You look just right. Trust me."

When Gram opened the door for Brand, his eyes darted

from her to Teddy, back to Gram, then back to Teddy. Teddy drew in a ragged breath. She had never seen a man look so splendid. His black tuxedo and bow tie made his streaked blond hair look lighter and his tan darker. His shoulders seemed wider and straighter, and his legs seemed to have grown an inch longer.

While Teddy had been looking Brand over he had been doing the same to her. Finally, his face turned from puzzlement to a happy laugh. "You look so beautiful you take my breath away," he said to Teddy. He still had a strange look on his face, though. Turning to Gram, he leaned way over and kissed her apricot cheek. "You look . . . happy tonight," he whispered in her ear.

She turned on him in mock indignation. "So I don't take your breath away! I have a mind to stay home, just for that."

Teddy and Gram stood in the middle of the bare room, ready to leave, but Brand hesitated. Teddy wondered what she was supposed to do, but decided to wait and see what he wanted. Finally he seemed to make a decision. "May I use your telephone?" he asked.

He went into the kitchen, where Teddy heard him cancelling a reservation. "All set," he said a few minutes later. "Let's be off."

They stopped a few minutes later at Denny's, where Teddy felt terribly overdressed, but the light and friendly atmosphere soon made her forget anything but the good food and company.

An hour later they climbed back into Brand's car and headed down the highway to their ranches. "I never had better steak, sonny," Gram growled from the back seat. "Thanks a lot. Been several years since I went out to eat."

Brand reached back and caught the tiny hand in his. "Glad

you came, Gram. You have a way of brightening the corner where you are, if I can steal a line from a song."

Brand went in when they arrived home and Gram took off to her bedroom. "Want to play a little gin?" Teddy asked.

Brand thought a moment. "We could. Or we could just talk, whichever you'd rather."

Teddy brought coffee and settled beside him on the couch. "Okay, talk," she instructed.

"I hope you weren't disappointed tonight when we went to Denny's."

Teddy smiled, remembering how she felt when she first went in. "Well, I did feel a little overdressed at first, but I soon forgot all about it. It was really nice. And the steaks were great."

He took her hand in his and patted it with his other one. "Do you know why we went there?"

"No, did we need a reason?"

He nodded. "I had reservations at Cyrano's, but I'd completely forgotten how Gram dresses up. I was afraid you'd be embarrassed at Denny's, but they wouldn't have let the little upstart in at Cyrano's. So I guess you'd say I was between a rock and a hard place."

Understanding flooded over Teddy, and a warm tender feeling for Brand came with it. How sweet and thoughtful!

"Anyway, your beautiful dress and even more beautiful you hasn't been wasted. I can't tell you how much pleasure I've had just looking at you tonight."

Teddy's eyes dropped and her face felt warm. "Thank you, Brand. I had a fantastic time, too. Really I did. And I noticed how gorgeous you look, too." She rolled her eyes. "What a shame, wasting all this gorgeousness on Denny's."

He leaned toward her and her heart nearly stopped. He

was going to kiss her and she had never wanted anything more. She turned her face up and closed her eyes. And waited. And waited. Teddy's blood boiled through her veins in anticipation. Finally, she peeped one eye open a bit.

Brand's face was about a foot from hers and he wore an expression of wonder. Then he lowered his lips to hers and they touched, as gently as a cloud drifting past. Her arms flew around his neck and pulled him closer. As his arms tightened around her, her reasoning left. What she wanted was for him to hold her close, and he did. Her hands did what they had been wanting to for as long as she could remember—they combed through the softest, blondest hair she had ever seen . . . or felt.

Then he pushed her away and she dropped to earth with no parachute. "I'm sorry. We shouldn't have done that."

"Why?" She thought for a moment, then she knew. Celia!

He smiled tenderly into her eyes and love shone from his brown eyes, reaching straight into her heart. "Have you forgotten, my little Teddy Bear?"

She nodded her head, feeling like a pushy child. "I remember. Celia."

"Celia?" A deep laugh rumbled from his broad chest. "Celia? No, Teddy, not Celia . . . Lynden. Your boyfriend, remember?"

nine

The next morning Gram studied Teddy's face. "You look as if you'd won the lottery, kitten," she said, dropping into her chair across the table.

"That's exactly how I feel, Gram. Brand kissed me last night. Oh, Gram, I *am* in love with him."

"Is he in love with you?"

Was he? He had not said so. "I don't know, Gram, but he kissed me."

Gram bowed her head and asked the blessing, filled both plates with eggs, bacon, and hash browns, then continued the conversation. "I couldn't be happier for you. As I told you before, I'm in love with Brand myself, but I want you to be careful. Men are strange creatures."

"But he only kissed me, Gram. A tender, gentle, beautiful kiss."

Gram spread apple butter on her toast and munched it as she drank her coffee. "All right. Just one more thing. You're absolutely certain he's not the one who robbed the bank on the other side of the Cascades?"

Ugh! Teddy had forgotten all about that. But she knew it was not Brand. There was not any hard evidence and it had been only a figment of Lynden's imagination. Brand would never do a thing like that. Never. "I'm sure, Gram, but I'll ask him right out one of these days. Like you said, nothing replaces good old communication."

As always, Lynden arrived to take them to church on

Sunday. "You look positively radiant this morning," he told Teddy. "That yellow dress matches the stars in your eyes."

Just then Gram came tearing out in her high-water jeans. She looked extra fancy too, in the crisp white shirt she had tucked into the pants. She motioned to Teddy and Lynden. "Come on, you slow pokes. We don't want to be late."

Brand came into the church soon after with Celia and a short, handsome, Mexican man with a wide smile and white, even teeth. Brand led them down the aisle to Teddy's pew and they all settled down. Brand reached for Teddy's hand and gave it one quick squeeze before gently replacing it in her lap. Nothing had ever felt so right to Teddy.

After church, Lynden went to the restroom and Brand brought the two strangers to Teddy. "I want you to meet Celia and Jesse Guitterres," he said. "And this is my love, Theodore Marland."

Lynden arrived on the scene just then.

"Glad to meet you folks," Teddy said. "I'm sure we'll see you again." She grabbed Lynden's hand and headed for his car with him in tow. Gram followed.

He turned the car around and threw gravel twenty feet as he tore out of the church yard. "I saw that turkey holding your hand, Teddy. I'd expect it of him but what's wrong with you?"

"We'll talk after we eat lunch," Teddy said calmly. "That is, if you're still eating with us?"

"What kind of question is that? Are you trying to get rid of me? If you are, just say so."

Teddy reached over the seat and put her hand on Lynden's arm. "I'm not trying to get rid of you. Let's just go home and eat, then we'll all have a good talk, all right?"

The roast tasted like cardboard to Teddy, and the potatoes

could have been balls of yarn, but eventually they finished eating and Gram left them alone.

"We've always agreed to be honest with each other, right?" she asked Lynden.

"Yeah. Is that what you called that performance in church?"

"Well, I really want you to be my good friend, but Brand and I have discovered we're more than that."

Lynden rewrapped his chocolate caramel and shoved the candy dish back onto the coffee table with a clatter. "So . . . you're more than friends. What are you?"

"We're . . . uh . . . I don't know what we are. We like each other a lot."

He sprang up from the couch. "I'm not going to sit still while that cowboy messes up your head. Just tell him to waddle on down the road."

Teddy grinned impulsively. "Too late, Lynden, my head's already messed up. My heart, too. The question now is whether you'll still be my friend."

He marched out of the kitchen, through the living room to the front door, with Teddy following. He opened the door, then turned back to her. "One thing you may have forgotten, he still has a price on his head. If you insist on this foolish behavior I may have to report his whereabouts to the authorities."

"Please don't do that," Teddy began, but the door slammed and Lynden was gone.

Ten seconds later he quietly opened the door and reached inside for his shoes. "Sorry," he said sheepishly, "I forgot these." This time he closed the door quietly.

Teddy dumped herself on the couch, and reached for the last remaining peanut butter kiss, feeling as though someone had kicked her in the stomach.

"Don't you worry about him," Gram said, when Teddy told her about Lynden's reaction. "But as I see it, you'd better learn for yourself what Brand has or hasn't done before Lynden blows the whistle."

"That could be easier said than done, Gram," Teddy said. She reached for a tissue and blew her nose.

The next morning, Teddy finished her breakfast and stepped outside when Brand rode up on Thunder. He dismounted, looped Thunder's reins around a small bush and opened his arms. Teddy ran into them and turned her lips up to receive his kiss. His wonderful kiss that turned her inside out and upside down and her knees into peppermint jelly.

"Well, didn't you get enough of that Saturday night?" a gravelly voice asked.

Teddy jerked away and faced her grandmother. "Hi, Gram. We were just saying hello."

"Some hello. What are we doing today, kitten?" She waved a gnarled old hand in their direction. "Besides that, I mean."

"We're fixing fences, Gram," Brand answered. "Could you possibly find something else to do? I mean, we both love you, but we have some private talking to do."

The tiny shoulders reared back and Gram wheeled around. "I can always find something to do when I'm not wanted." Teddy detected a twinkle in Gram's caustic words. "Okay, my little Teddy Bear, let's get busy." He collected the box of spike nails and the four-pound hammer and headed for the south pasture. They worked together, reassembling the fence and replacing logs that were too far gone.

"How am I ever going to repay you for all this work?"

Teddy asked after a while.

Brand flashed a joyful smile. "What a short memory you have. You already repaid me, or should I say, Brutus and Caesar paid your debt?"

"That wasn't anything. It took only a couple of hours. I plan to pay hour for hour. Not that my hours are worth as much as yours, since you're so much stronger."

"Well, I have an idea. Why don't we have an instant replay of our dinner out the other night?" He hesitated. "Minus Gram?"

"Sure, I'd like that. And Gram wouldn't mind a bit. Although she told me several weeks ago that she's in love with you."

"She didn't mean it."

"Well, not like me." Teddy gasped. *What had she just said? Maybe Brand would not notice.*

But Brand did notice. He jerked upright and the log he was holding dropped to the ground. His brown eyes shot stars. "So, Teddy Bear, you're in love with me, huh?"

Teddy's face burned. Never had it felt so hot. "I meant like I would . . . you know . . . she's older."

Brand took her in his arms and held her tenderly. His lips brushed hers. "I know she's older, but that wasn't what you said." He pulled away and looked into her eyes, laughing. "Teddy Bear, I was going to ask you to marry me the night we went to Cyrano's." He lowered his head and proceeded to kiss her thoroughly. When he released her they both breathed in ragged gasps. "But I don't see how I can wait that long. I want to marry you, and soon, my little love."

They sat down on the ground to talk. Somehow she had to make sure he was exactly what he appeared. "You're way ahead of yourself," Teddy said. "We don't even know each other. I may have some deep dark secret in my past and for all I know, you may have a whole closet full of skeletons."

Brand quieted and became serious. "I already have yours figured out, and I don't have any, so what's to learn?"

"Mine? What do you have figured out about me?"

"Your mother died when you were born? That's why Gram named you. I didn't push because I know it makes you sad. Your blue blue eyes are so beautiful when you're happy. They're pretty with tears in them, too, but I'd rather make them laugh."

Oh. Her mother. She had forgotten all about that. In a way that was a deep dark secret she did not want him to know about. But she would worry about that another time. Right now, she must not be diverted. She had to learn where he got the money to buy his ranch. "What I was trying to do, was find out if you had some secret in your past that we should talk about."

He nodded. "Okay. No, I don't have any secrets you should know. Satisfied?"

"What about any that I shouldn't know?"

He studied her face a moment. "Are you asking about the women in my life?"

"If there were any you want to tell me about."

He shook his head. His sun-streaked hair fluffed back and forth, looking so soft and bouncy that Teddy wanted to run her fingers through it and forget all about skeletons.

"One thing I've wondered about—where did you dig up enough money to buy your ranch? That's a lot of wampum for a guy your age."

For a fraction of a second he looked stricken, then recovered. "Well," he drawled, "I've been digging a good long time. Sure enough, after I kept at it long enough, I found the money."

"But where, Brand?"

He looked mysteriously. "In a secret place where no one else on God's green earth could look."

Teddy watched Brand's face . . . and waited. But he did not say anymore. "Okay, buster," she said, mimicking Gram's gravelly voice, "get to work if you expect a paycheck on Friday."

They laughed and went back to work. But Teddy did not feel quite satisfied. One thing was certain. If he had done something so terrible as robbing a bank he would tell her at this point in their relationship. Wait! What was she thinking? Of course, he would . . . not. Anyone who would rob a bank would not hesitate to lie about it. She would have to ask him point blank and watch his face. But what a horrible thing to ask a man who had just proposed marriage.

She decided to forget the whole thing and just enjoy the new relationship for a while. Her first love. They continued repairing fences together for the next three days and enjoyed it as much as though they were on wild and romantic excursions together.

Then, one evening, Lynden called sounding a lot less then friendly. "You'd better read the paper tonight."

"I always read the paper, Lynden. Is there something you want me to see?"

"Yeah. On the inside of the front page. It's coming into the open, Teddy." A loud crash, then a dial tone told Teddy he had finished the conversation.

"What a rude pig," Teddy said aloud, reaching for the evening paper. She opened it to the second page and folded it over so she would be sure to find the article. She already knew what it was and it did not take long to find, nor to read. Just a small item about the not-so-recent bank robbery, stating the date, the details of the robbery, a description of the man, the rig he escaped in—a black 1984 truck with a winch in front—and that the Eugene police department had reason to believe the man had settled down in the Bend area.

Teddy dropped the paper on the floor and collapsed on the couch, trembling. The description matched Brand right down to the Stetson he always wore. And the description of the truck sounded exactly like the one Brand drove around the ranch. She lay there, trying not to think, until Gram came in and found her. Then, she gathered up the paper and showed it to the old lady.

After reading the article through, Gram sat down on the couch and gathered the top half of Teddy's five-foot, eight-inch frame into her arms as though she were still a baby. "I'm sorry, kitten," she crooned, rocking back and forth. "It isn't a nice situation, but you're going to have to find out. Why don't you show him the paper and tell him about Lynden's insinuations?"

Teddy nodded. "I'll have to do that. I'll just have to." She rounded up the scissors and cut out the notice. Twenty minutes later, the now familiar attack on the door jolted both women.

"Hey, do I have a great idea!" Brand said, pulling off his boots and hurrying to the bathroom to wash his hands. Then he took Teddy into his arms for a gentle, but thorough, kiss. He draped an arm over her shoulder and steered her back to the kitchen where Gram still sat. He leaned over and kissed the old woman on her wrinkled cheek. "How's my favorite Gram this evening?" he whispered into her ear.

She reached up a small hand and imprisoned his larger one on her shoulder. "Flattery will get you everywhere," she said.

Brand dropped to the couch and patted the place beside him. When Teddy complied, he continued. "I have to go visit my folks this weekend and I want you to go along." His eyes never left hers. "What do you think?" he finally asked.

What did she think? It sounded exactly like the opportunity she had been waiting for. Surely she could not spend a weekend with Brand's family without finding out something about his history, good or bad. And she would be able to postpone confronting him with her clipping until after the trip.

ten

"Well, what do you think?" he repeated.

"It sounds like fun," Teddy said, "but why would you want me to go to your folks's place?"

He seemed so excited he could barely sit still. "I want to show you off to them. And I want you to meet them, too."

Gram had been sitting quietly. "Go on, kitten," she finally said, "it'll be good for you."

Gram! Teddy could not leave her alone to care for the llamas. "I'd like to, really I would," she began. "I almost said yes, but I forgot you, Gram. I can't go off and leave you with all the work."

"Pish posh. We have it all caught up. I'll just feed and water. That'll leave me most of the day to get into trouble."

"I can send Rolf over to help," Brand suggested. "He isn't always busy, either."

"You send Rolf over with Pharaoh, if you're so intent on helping," the little woman said, laughing.

"I'll do that. With instructions to ride with you. Now, Teddy Bear, there's nothing to stop us."

But Gram was not finished. "Don't you dare tell him to ride with me, sonny. My death wish isn't to be shot by a jealous wife."

But Brand had Teddy in his arms and they did not hear Gram's old joke.

When the sun awakened Saturday morning, it found Brand and Teddy crossing the Cascade Mountains, excited to be together. Teddy had a doubt or two about the integrity of her spy trip, but she told herself she would just enjoy herself, meeting his family and getting to know Brand better. After all, he had asked her to marry him. She had not given him an answer but the offer was still good as far as she knew.

They talked nonstop as they drove through the beautiful forests and paused at several waterfalls on the Clear Lake Highway. Then they drove out of the trees, through Springfield, and into Eugene. "My folks live about a mile out on River Road," Brand explained as he expertly threaded through the dense traffic of the large city.

Ten minutes later they drove up to a neat, white, two-story house surrounded by tall firs and pines. The front door opened and Brand's parents ran down the steps to engulf him in their arms. As they all talked at once, asking how each had been, Teddy could not help but notice the close relationship, and how happy Brand and his parents were to be together again.

Then Brand remembered Teddy and hauled her to his side. "I almost forgot to tell you I brought someone along." Brand introduced them, and assured them he had a nice little Teddy Bear.

Brand's mother, Donna, had lunch ready and they gathered around the little table on the north porch. "Tell us about Teddy, and how you met her," Brand's father, Frank, suggested.

Brand winked at Teddy. "I met her when she tried to steal my water. Water's semiprecious over there."

"He tried to smash the door out of our house, he was so mad," Teddy added, laughing.

"Then she tried to lay the blame on an innocent animal," Brand continued, his eyes taking on a dreamy look as he remembered.

Teddy pounded him on the shoulder. "You saw her do it."

"All right, you two," Frank said, laughing, "there won't be any dessert until you get this all straightened out."

Brand stopped short. "Dessert? Well, I guess Iris was the water thief, but we fixed her wagon. But then those crazy llamas broke down the fence and invaded my ranch."

"Llamas?" Brand's parents yelled together.

Brand laughed. "Yes, llamas. She raises llamas next door to my cattle ranch." He shrugged. "There goes the neighborhood, but what can a guy do?" His eyes twinkled at Teddy. "But she's making so much money she chooses not to shear their wool, whereby she could make another $80,000 a year."

"Gram's with you, Brand. She thinks we should shear them but I just can't do it," Teddy said.

The little group visited through the rest of lunch, Frank and Donna learning something about the two ranches and also about Teddy and her grandmother.

"Well, what would you like to do while you're here?" Frank asked when they had finished eating.

"See the ocean?" Teddy piped up before Brand had a chance.

A happy smile spread over Brand's tanned face. "I'll bet you haven't been to the coast too many times."

Teddy willed her face to stay nice and white. "Well, I'm embarrassed to tell you, but I've never seen the ocean. Gram and I just stay home and work."

Brand nodded his head. "Hmmm. So that's why you came, is it?" he asked in mock seriousness.

Frank laughed loudly. "Can't think of a better reason if the girl hasn't seen the Pacific yet. Let's do that in the morning. But what about today?"

Brand turned to Teddy and nodded, then raised his hands several times in front of him, as though pulling information from her. "Come on, out with it. Surely you have our itinerary all planned."

"Okay." She turned to face Donna. "I want to learn all about Brand. All the good things he's ever done, and also the bad. I want to leave here knowing the total man."

"Unfair!" Brand protested. "I've never done anything good, and I don't want you knowing the bad, so let's not get into that. I'll just have to keep you so busy you forget all about that idea. I was thinking we might go out for dinner tonight. Maybe The North Bank?"

"Great, and I'll bet you want to take Teddy out to the ranch this afternoon," Frank said. "We've been helping the new owners a lot, so we're sure of being welcome."

Donna showed Teddy to her room at the head of the stairs. "You have your own matching bath through this door," Donna said, opening a narrow door into a sunshiny, yellow bathroom. Then she pulled back the gold-specked white drapes in the bedroom, revealing a sliding glass door opening onto a private balcony facing the backyard.

"What a gorgeous home," Teddy said.

"Thank you. We had it redone before we moved in." She left Teddy alone to put her things away. Teddy had not brought an evening dress, but she had a nice short one. A light green chiffon, which she hung up so the wrinkles could hang out while they ran to the ranch.

The ranch looked a lot like Brand's. Hereford cattle dotted the green pastures as far as the eye could see, and the buildings showed excellent maintenance. Teddy looked into Brand's shining eyes. "It's as nice as your ranch," she said softly.

He swallowed and reached for her hand. "At least." She knew at that moment how much he had loved this beautiful place, and how many memories it had given him. And instinctively she knew that his Central Oregon ranch was an attempt at a replay. How she would love to help him make a million memories of their own.

After they left the ranch in Alvadore they drove past Fern Ridge Lake where Brand swam and canoed as a boy. Then they hurried home to prepare for the evening.

Later, Brand's eyes lit up with joy when Teddy came down the stairs in her mint chiffon dress. She had pulled her dark hair all to one side, letting it fall in a cascade of curls.

"Don't you think we make a fantastic pair?" Brand asked his mother as they drove downtown to the restaurant.

"You look beautiful together, yes, but are you a pair?" Donna answered, her eyebrows raised questioningly.

Brand looked at Teddy. She returned his gaze, saying nothing and feeling everything. Finally, he looked back at his mother, grinned foolishly and shrugged. "I don't know, Mom, I'm working on it."

Back home, after a wonderfully impressive dinner, everyone changed and Donna served coffee. "Well," Teddy said, "this must be the time for my education. Tell me all about Brand."

Donna sipped her coffee, slipping off into some other time and place. After a moment she returned. "Brand was the best kid anyone ever had. He may have told you that we were almost middle-aged when we married, so he was an only child. He's been a wonderful son. Sometimes during the years, we'd forget who was the child and who were the parents. We've all taken care of each other."

"You mean he never got into trouble?" Teddy asked,

trying to bring anything she should know into the open.

"No, but he should have, a couple of times," Frank volunteered. "Remember the time you lambasted that guy with potatoes, Brand?"

Brand slapped his hand against his forehead. "He never forgets. He's like an elephant. I swear he is. I'd forgotten all about it. Dad had sent me to the dump to get rid of several sacks of rotting potatoes. It was dark and I started heaving them down into the dump. Then I saw this flashlight down there, where someone was evidently gleaning—strictly against the rules. I just happened to start throwing in that direction, and you never saw a flashlight come out of a hole so fast."

Everyone laughed at the memory. "Tell me more." Teddy said when everyone quieted down.

"How about the times he skipped the Boy Scouts to go see a girl?" Frank asked, and roared with laughter.

Now! This sounded interesting. She might as well learn about the girls in his life.

"That was nothing," Brand said, laughing. "I was only fifteen at the time and after about the third time, the leader discovered me missing. He went next door to the girl's house after me and raised such a stink the girl never spoke to me again."

"And the blind date that you couldn't handle at first sight? Remember, what you told her?" Frank threw back his gray head and laughed heartily again.

"Dad! How many more of these incidents do you have ready to zap at me?"

"Go on, son, tell Teddy how you got out of that date," Donna said. She laughed too, remembering days gone by. Obviously very precious days. Teddy could see they both felt intense pride in their only child.

"Well . . . I'm not going to do it. You don't have to testify against yourself even in a court of law." Brand winked at Teddy, got up and took her arm. "We're going to check on the moon. We'll talk to you when you've found a new subject." He took Teddy to the sliding glass door and they stepped out into a silver fairyland.

"Oh Brand, it's nice out here," Teddy said, taking in the small waterfalls and stream that occupied center stage in a perfectly groomed backyard.

"Yeah, and even the moon is trying. It's getting toward full. Come over here and sit with me."

They sat on a stone and wrought iron bench beside the waterfalls. The sound of the falls and bubbling creek, together with the fragrance of roses, petunias, and alyssum, and the moon spilling silver beams over everything in sight, made an even more romantic ambiance than the restaurant had. When Brand pulled Teddy to him, she lay her head on his shoulder, drinking in the beauty and peacefulness of the night. His spicy aftershave blended with the other smells, a few crickets added their music to the evening, and Teddy decided she could stay just like this forever.

"I love you, Teddy," he whispered. "You look and smell like my own special heaven." He put his hand under her chin and turned it up. The moment his lips touched hers, Teddy heard her own heavenly music and felt a bright pink cloud settling down over them, protecting them from any harshness of reality.

She knew she loved him. And she also knew he could never have done anything immoral, unethical, or illegal, let alone rob a bank. As he repeated the kiss, she lay in his arms, enjoying it to the fullest.

"Anyone out here?" Frank's piercing voice broke the magic and Teddy sat up with a guilty jerk, looking toward the sound.

Brand said something unintelligible under his breath before he answered. "We're out here by the waterfalls."

Donna and Frank stepped out of the trees into the moonlight, then settled onto the other bench beside the water. They sat outside for an hour getting acquainted and watching the moon flitting in and out of small white clouds. Finally, Brand put his arms around Teddy again. "You're cold," he said against her cheek. "I'm taking you inside."

Frank and Donna followed and Teddy gave up all hopes of being alone with Brand. She visited a while longer and went to bed.

Before sleep came, Teddy lay in the comfortable bed and went over the afternoon and evening. Frank and Donna were certainly ready to welcome her into the family. And Brand seemed to have been the ideal child. If he had ever done anything wrong his parents did not know about it. The family was far too frank and open to be concealing anything major. They had put every doubt to rest—not that she had ever had any.

She jerked away when she heard a voice, but fell right back to sleep. Then she heard it again and opened her eyes. Sunlight streamed through the sheer curtain at the window and Brand's voice and gentle knock drew her to consciousness.

"Good morning, my fairy princess," Brand said in his endearing way. "I'm waking you for breakfast. We need to get with it if we're going to the coast this morning." He seemed to pause outside her door and then turned and walked down the hallway.

Teddy showered quickly and climbed into white pants and a red sweater. She would rather have worn jeans, but Brand saw her in those every day of his life. She would like to look somewhat special today. She put her hair in two ponytails, each with a red ribbon, added a touch of red lipstick, and ran down the stairs.

The family sat at the table drinking coffee while waiting for her. "Wow," Frank said, when he saw her, "this girl isn't old enough to be so far from her mother."

Brand got up and put his arms around Teddy and kissed her tenderly, then seated her at the table beside him. He grinned at his father. "You're almost right, Dad. She's twenty-one."

Donna served waffles with strawberries and ice cream for breakfast. "They'll stay with you until we get around to eating lunch," she said.

Then they all jumped into Brand's car and took off for the coast. Teddy barely heard the conversation, so eager was she to see the ocean.

Brand laughed at her preoccupation. "You won't see the ocean for nearly an hour, so you may as well enjoy the trip." Even though it was only the last part of August, lots of trees showed golden, orange and red colors.

Finally, they left the mountains and, in a little while, drove through Florence, a busy little coastal town situated almost in the exact middle of Oregon's coastline. Teddy watched for the ocean, but did not see it until they almost drove into it. Bright blue, as far as she could see, with glittering silver stars where the sunbeams kissed the waves. The waves rolled in perfect symmetry until they neared the shore, where they burst into wildly foaming water and crashed onto the sandy beach. Brand jumped out, ran around, pulled Teddy from the car, and hugged her to him.

The wind snatched at Teddy's hair and stung her eyes. And she could not tell whether the enormous roar she heard was the wind or the ocean, or both. Then Frank and Donna got out of the back, allowing the door to slam against the car with a force that made Teddy jump.

"Wow, I've never felt wind this strong," she said, closing her eyes against the sand that blew into her face with tremendous force.

Brand opened the car and retrieved everyones' sweaters. All of them took off their shoes and put them into the car.

"The sand feels wonderful on my feet," Teddy said, "but stings my face. Do you think we can walk in this hurricane?"

Brand took her hand and started toward the roaring ocean. "Sure, we can walk. It always blows this way down here." When they neared the ocean they turned and walked along the beach, watching the waves creep ever farther onto the sand. When a super big wave burst a few feet from them, Brand shoved Teddy into it.

Teddy had not expected that. She screamed and jumped into Brand's arms, pulling her feet up from the now-receding water. "That stuff's cold," she yelled above the roar. "It should have icebergs in it."

Brand laughed and carried her back from the water a little way and set her on her feet. "Roll up your pants," he commanded, doing the same with his own. "We're going wading. You'll be surprised how soon the water loses its cool."

They continued walking south, following the curve of the beach. Sometimes they walked in the shallow, foaming waves and sometimes they plodded along in the wet sand.

Teddy did not care, as long as Brand held her hand.

"Are we going any place special, or just walking?" Teddy asked after about a mile.

He nodded. "We're going to the jetty. It's fun to walk on, and we can check out the fishermen."

In a little while they walked the length of the jetty, watching the waves crash into the rocks, sending twenty-foot walls of water flying into the china-blue sky. "Where are your folks?" Teddy asked when they climbed down from the mammoth structure.

Brand grinned and shrugged. "Who knows? Want to hide from them?"

"Of course not. They love you and want to spend this time with you." They both had to shout, for the wind tried to snatch away every sound while the ocean joined in, roaring out its mighty strength.

"Okay, let's go back," Brand yelled into her ear. They walked hand in hand as they retraced their steps over the two-mile distance.

Brand drove to Devil's Elbow for lunch. Mountains on three sides protected the much smaller beach from the wind. They took off their sweaters to enjoy the meal while watching the ever-changing ocean.

"Are you ready to go home?" Frank asked after they tossed the remnants of the food to the sea gulls and put the other things back into the car.

"I guess," Brand answered. "I really wanted Teddy to see the sun set over the ocean, but we still have to drive home."

Brand packed their things into the car as soon as they got back to his folks's place. It would be midnight when they reached their farms.

Frank and Donna walked out to the car to tell the young

people goodbye. "How'd you like the ocean, Teddy?" Donna asked.

"I loved it. I can't wait to see it again," Teddy bubbled.

A wide smile split Frank's face. "Of course you liked it," he grinned impishly. "That's why Brand takes all his women there."

eleven

Donna smacked Frank on the arm. "His ex-girlfriends, you idiot," she said, laughing. "And I don't remember him ever taking anyone else to the coast. You're just trying to make the poor girl jealous."

"I'm trying to help her see that Brand's a good catch," he said.

"I give the girl credit for having good sense," Donna said. "Why don't we let her discover how nice he is all by herself? That's part of the thrill of finding each other, remember?"

Brand sat comfortably in his bucket seat grinning at both of his parents, neither embarrassed nor upset in the least. He started the car and stuck his head out the window for a last kiss from first his mother, then his father. He pushed the gearshift down and eased away. "You guys come see us real soon," he called as they glided into the street.

Teddy leaned back and closed her eyes. She had learned all she would from this trip. A lot—and all good.

Brand slipped his hand over hers. "What do you think of my family?"

"I like them a lot. It sort of made me think about. . . ." She had been thinking about her mother and father. No, not her own mother and father, but how her life might have been if she had had a mother and father around for her. Now, how could she have even thought that? Gram had done her very best for her all the time. "They sure like you a lot," she finished.

"Not any more than Gram likes you." He stroked her hand

with his thumb. "You were about to say it made you think about your mom and dad, weren't you? Wouldn't you like to talk about your folks, little Teddy Bear?"

She did not answer, but shook her head. She knew Brand wanted to comfort her, but her parentage was one subject that would always stay buried, as far as she was concerned. She searched for a subject strong enough to drive the other one out of his mind. "Do you really take all your women to the coast?"

Brand signaled, then turned off the freeway onto the McKenzie Highway, laid his head back on his headrest and laughed. His laugh sounded almost like Frank's, only more refined. "You're the first one ever, and I'm glad. It was special to me, introducing you to the ocean."

"Me, too. I want to go back, Brand."

"On our honeymoon?"

She burst out laughing, feeling a great relief. He really wanted to marry her. "So you didn't take your women to the coast. Where did you take them?"

He hesitated a moment, then glanced her way. His lips twitched and his brown eyes sparkled pure gold. "Oh, I usually took them to dark, quiet places."

Teddy knew he was kidding but could not respond.

"Hey, why the silence," he asked a moment later. "Do you love me so much you can't stand the idea of me ever having had another girlfriend?"

She nodded.

He reached for her hand again. "To tell the truth I haven't had that many girlfriends, and no serious ones. I was always too busy studying or helping Mom and Dad on the ranch. As I got older, so did they, and at the last I worked from dawn to dusk." He chuckled. "You know, like we both do now."

"Do you care about my other boyfriends?" she asked mischievously.

He slowed for a bird eating something from the roadside snow, then resumed his speed. "Not a bit."

She tossed his hand back into his own lap. "What a thing to say! You could at least act a little jealous, couldn't you?"

His hand slid into hers once more. "You can't even imagine how jealous I'd be if I had a reason. I'd tear any man apart who touched you now, and maybe any that ever had." He retrieved his hand to negotiate a sharp upward curve, as they drove into the mountains. Teddy's eyes met his, and saw love in them that made her stomach flutter.

They talked about everything and laughed about anything as they drove through the mountains, then over the open country to their ranches. Much too soon, Brand carried Teddy's suitcases into the old run-down ranch house. He set them down in the empty living room, kissed her goodbye, and disappeared through the front door.

"Well, get those shoes off and tell me about your trip," said Gram.

"He isn't the one, Gram. They're really great people. And I love him, and—" Then it hit her like a spiked volleyball. Gram might not feel quite so happy about her new love. What would they do with Gram?

"That's what I needed to know," Gram said. "Of course, we both knew he was all right, but now we're sure." She glanced at the clock on the stove. "Do you see what time it is? Those fool llamas will be ready for breakfast at five o'clock no matter what time we want to go to bed."

The clock read twelve-thirty when Teddy crawled into her bed, tired, but exhilarated as she had never been. She set her alarm for quarter of five in the morning. But she could not seem to fall asleep. *Father,* she prayed silently, *won't You please help me know for sure if You want me to marry Brand. If for any reason You don't, could You please make me feel uneasy about it when I wake up? Thank you, Father. I love You. Good night.*

Teddy turned off the alarm at the first chirp, and jumped out of bed, feeling as high as a cloud and just as fluffy. Brand loved her and they would be married! And best and most important of all, God wanted her to marry him!

She left the house quietly so she would not awaken Gram, but Teddy found her in the barn, loading feed onto the pickup. "Gram, did you forget I'm back?" Teddy asked, laughing from pure happiness.

Gram's yellow-gray curls shook. "Naw, but I thought you might be tired."

"I'm too happy to be tired." Teddy told Gram more about her trip as they fed the llamas together.

Brand did not show up all day and Teddy thought she would go wild if she did not see him soon. She could not bring herself to leave Gram to go to his place, and she felt a little shy, anyway. He would come as soon as possible.

As Teddy and Gram sat down to supper, he arrived in his sports car and they invited him to eat with them.

"I hear you're in love with my girl." Gram's granite voice made it sound as if he had stolen the crown jewels.

He buttered a hot biscuit and spread honey over it, then nodded soberly. "I'm in love with both of you, Gram. Right now, I'm trying to figure out how to get us all into the same family. Teddy hasn't said yes yet. Would I have better luck with you?"

Gram swallowed a big bite of corn she had just chewed off

the cob. Then she waved the cob at Brand. "No, you have to deal with her, but I'll push while you pull."

Brand flew off his chair as though catapulted. Forgetting all about his uneaten supper, he grabbed Teddy from her chair, wrapped his arms around her and danced wildly around the room. Finally, he fell to the couch with her still in his arms. "That's it, baby, there's nothing to stop us." He kissed her quickly, then looked into her eyes. "Say it, Teddy Bear, say you'll marry me."

Teddy got to her feet, then cast an impish glance at Brand. "Sorry about that tornado that just blew through. Shall we finish eating now?"

Brand jerked her back down beside him and crushed her in his arms. "This is going to get tighter until you say the word." He pecked her on the cheek, then tightened his grip.

"This is nice," she said. He tightened his arms again and she struggled for breath. "How come you've never hugged me like this before?" she wheezed.

He squeezed her again, then released her and tweaked a curl gently. "I can't hurt you, even though you're a brat," he said. "I give up." He started toward the door. "I'll just go find someone else."

Teddy followed Brand to the door and told him goodbye. As he climbed into his car she called to him. "If you can't find anyone else who'll marry you, I guess I could. You know what they say, it's a dirty job but someone has to do it."

He piled out of the car and raced to the house with the speed of sound, hitting the steps like a bolt of lightning. He went through the third one with the crack of thunder—sprawling all the way to the top. Teddy dropped to her knees on the porch so she could look into his face. "Are you all right?"

He winked at her. "I don't know. If I could get my busted leg out of the step I might be able to tell."

After resting a few minutes, he managed to haul the leg out and, leaning on Teddy's shoulder, he managed to hop back into the kitchen. Before leaving the porch, he looked back at the mangled steps. "I suppose you're going to sue me for wrecking your steps."

When Teddy had Brand seated comfortably on the couch, he pulled a small package from his shirt pocket and laid it on the coffee table. "So you're going to do it, huh?"

"Marry you? Was there ever any doubt?"

He pointed to the small box. "Well, that's for you, but not until you feed me the rest of my supper."

Teddy reached for the box but Brand grabbed her hand and held it firmly. "Not until I've had my supper," he repeated.

"I just wanted to look at it, and see how heavy it is," she said.

"After my supper."

Gram jumped up, refilled Brand's plate with warm food, fixed two more biscuits and filled his coffee cup with steaming brew. Then she put the plate into his eager hands. But he took his time eating.

"Does your leg hurt much?" Teddy asked fifteen minutes later. Food still covered half his plate.

"Only when you get too near that little package on the coffee table."

Teddy helped Gram with the dishes. At least it kept her busy and away from the package. Her hands flew. Maybe she could get all through before Brand finished his food.

"Could I have some more biscuits, please?"

Teddy buttered and honeyed two more of Gram's fluffy golden biscuits, carried them over and dropped them onto

Brand's plate, then turned and tried to snatch the box. But Brand's uninjured foot flashed over the package, covering it neatly and so strongly she could not dislodge it. Teddy gave up and continued with the dishes.

"I need another ear of corn, please?"

What was this? Teddy had never seen Brand eat like this. And with an injured foot? He was probably getting even for her own mischief. Well, she could outfox a fox, any day of the week.

"Could you fix Brand's corn, Gram?" she asked. "I have to go feed the llamas. I'll be back in about an hour and a half."

"No, don't go." Brand jumped to his feet—and fell over again. Teddy ran and helped him back onto the couch.

"You did hurt yourself," she said trying to make him comfortable.

His face had paled somewhat under his dark tan, but his mouth spread in a wide laugh. "No, just trying to get attention. Now, are you ready to open this little box?" Teddy leaned over and kissed him as he put the long-awaited box into her hand.

Sitting on the couch beside him, she unwrapped the blue foil from a lightweight cardboard box. Hmm, not exactly what she had expected, but there must be another box inside this one. She carefully opened the lid and pulled out—a feathery fish hook? Disappointment flooded over her like ocean waves, breaking and spilling until she felt about as tall as a grain of sand.

twelve

Then wild laughter caught her attention. "I must have given you the wrong box," he said laughing some more.

When she looked into his love-filled eyes, he pulled her to him and kissed her softly, then again, not quite so softly. Her heart started beating again and she found she could not breathe. He pulled out another box, this one covered with red foil, and laid it in her hand.

She looked into his eyes. He nodded silently and smiled. When she pulled the foil away, she held a royal blue, felt-covered jeweler's box in her hand. This was it! If she could just hold her hands steady enough to open the box! She fumbled a moment before a strong hand took it, opened it, and put it back into her hand.

There it was, winking at her! The most beautiful diamond she had ever seen, nestled in soft, red velvet. She felt hypnotized, unable to take her eyes from it. Then, a single tear formed in her left eye. Why would she cry now? At the happiest moment of her life. She blinked it away, and started laughing. "Oh, Brand, thank you, thank you. Gram! Come see it."

"I've already seen it, kitten."

"How could that be? I've only seen it, now."

Brand took the box from her and lifted the ring from its velvet nest. "Let's see if it fits, Teddy Bear." He took her left hand and slipped the ring onto her third finger—a perfect fit.

Teddy looked at the ring sparkling on her finger then threw her arms around his neck and kissed him. "It fits perfectly," she said a little later while they all ate the cake and ice cream Hannah and Rolf had brought in response to Brand's call. The decorated cake had *Congratulations Brand and Teddy* written on it in pink letters.

"Somehow everyone knew about this little party but me," Teddy said laughing. "But how did you know my ring size? As if I didn't know. You traitor, Gram."

"He got your ring some time ago," Gram said, "so of course I had to see it. I sent the first one back. It was too small." Gram's faded old eyes twinkled. "The diamond, I mean," she finished, cackling over her joke.

"What am I getting myself into?" Brand asked no one in particular. "Two women, and they're both determined to give me a bad time."

After a while, Teddy looked out the window and noticed darkness settling around them. "We're through opening presents, we're all stuffed on ice cream and cake, I wonder what we're supposed to be doing now," she mused aloud.

"Dreaming, I guess, my little Teddy Bear. Dreaming about tomorrow and the rest of our tomorrows."

Hannah and Rolf stayed until it was bedtime for everyone so Brand kissed Teddy goodbye while they all watched, and then went home.

Gram and Teddy returned to the kitchen to relax a few minutes and rehash the evening. Teddy's blue eyes radiated happiness. "Oh, Gram, I never thought I could be so happy," she said, almost purring.

"I'm glad. You've missed enough in your life. You deserve somebody special, and for my money you got him."

Teddy dropped a kiss on the withered old cheek. "Don't say that, Gram. You've been everything to me."

Gram smiled and her old eyes twinkled with merriment.

"Until the handsome prince kissed you. I thought he never would, after that toad messed you up." Then she became serious. "Have you decided which ranch you'll live on? I'm sure his is a lot nicer."

"We haven't talked about that at all, Gram. Now we'd better get to bed, and you sleep in a little late in the morning. I'll do the early chores."

Teddy had barely finished her chores the next morning and sat down to Gram's good breakfast, when Brand limped into the house with a newspaper in his hand. "I took off my shoes, Gram," he said walking to the sink to wash his hands.

"Sit down and have some breakfast," Gram said, putting on another plate.

Brand waited until after Gram asked the blessing to tell them what he had found in the paper. "It's a little announcement about the county fair, coming up next week. We could go if you want. Let's go over to Redmond today and buy tickets for it."

"Sounds like fun," Teddy said.

After they bought the tickets in Redmond, they stopped at an ice cream store for a peanut butter parfait before going home. "Have you thought about Gram?" Teddy asked while they ate their cool treats.

"Lots of times. Why?"

"I mean what am I going to do with her when we get married?"

Brand laid his spoon down and swallowed. "What kind of question is that? What did you plan to do with her?" He almost sounded indignant.

Teddy shrugged, embarrassed. "I don't know exactly. That's why I'm trying to talk to you about it."

Brand picked up his spoon and shoved in a huge bite of the ice cream confection, chewed and swallowed, before he spoke. "I don't even know where we're going to live yet, do you?"

Teddy shook her head.

He continued as though he had not stopped. "But wherever we live, she'll live with us." His eyes softened. "I asked you both, remember?"

A fantastic peace flooded throughout Teddy's being. She should have known. "Brand, have I told you how terribly much I love you? You've just made me love you a tiny bit more, and I didn't think that was possible."

They finished their treats and drove home. "Do you think Gram's worrying about what we'll do with her?" Brand asked as they let themselves into the house and took off their shoes.

"I don't know. Let's talk to her right away, just in case."

In a few minutes Gram came in the back door. She had already shed her shoes and washed up in the utility room.

Brand took Gram's small hand in his. "Gram, we've been thinking. Where would you like to live after we're married?"

A small cloud passed over her face, but the sun broke through and her happy smile showed only the slightest hesitation. "I guess it's up to you two. The ranch is Teddy's, you know. If you're going to live on your place, maybe I could just stay here. Otherwise, I can get an apartment in Bend."

"No way," Brand said, stroking the frail hand he still held. "Where we go, you go. I was just wondering where you think that ought to be."

Gram shook her head. "I wouldn't feel right about that. Young people should be alone."

"Don't you give it a thought," Brand said. "And wherever we end up, I promise I'll check my boots at the door—and wash my hands quickly. Actually, I think it's a good idea."

A couple of days later Brand arrived with a small trailer behind his pickup. Teddy dropped her hoe and went to meet him. After his usual hug and warm kiss he stepped over to the trailer. "I'll bet you can't guess what I have inside."

Gram threw her hoe down and joined Teddy at the high-sided trailer. "Open this thing before we rip it apart," Gram instructed as Brand stepped to the back of the truck and unfastened the tailgate.

"It isn't alive," he informed the two women as he lifted the wood section out and placed it on the ground.

"Oooh," they said in unison when they saw a bright blue bicycle inside. A tandem bicycle.

Brand put a strong arm around Gram and pulled her close. "Sorry, Gram, I couldn't find a bicycle built for three."

"It's okay. We can take turns."

Brand unloaded the long bicycle and motioned for Teddy to climb onto the rear seat. He straddled the front. "Let's take it for a spin, Teddy Bear."

Teddy threw back her shoulders. "Aren't you being the least tiny bit chauvinistic? Maybe I want to ride in front."

Brand laughed. "I wasn't being a pig, at least not purposely. Okay, we'll do it right. How much do you weigh?"

"That's a sneaky way to learn my weight."

"The people at the bike shop said the heavier has to ride in front." Brand raised his chin a couple of inches. "And I might add that he's the captain."

Teddy laughed and gave his shoulder a small shove. "You made that all up. So . . . what is the other person called?"

"I didn't make it up, Teddy, really. The back person is called the stoker, and they said this is a neat place because this person can eat lunch or most anything he wants to. But the captain absolutely must tell the stoker when they're coming to a bump or corner or stop sign." He raised his right hand to his forehead and executed a smart salute. "Got it, stoker baby?"

"Got it." She climbed onto the bike.

"Ready?" the captain yelled. "One, two, three, blastoff." He gave a hard push with his foot and they were riding down the driveway. Wobbly, but riding.

"Wow, this is different!" Teddy yelled. By the time they reached the highway, they were moving so fast it frightened Teddy. "I'm scared," she yelled.

"I'm braking," he returned. "We're slowing for the corner." After they negotiated the corner, they picked up speed again.

In a little while Teddy felt comfortable and sat back, releasing the handlebars. "If only I had my knitting," she yelled.

"You won't have to knit your own clothes, anymore," he said. "I plan to buy you the most beautiful wardrobe in the world—to match you."

"Idiot!" she screamed into the wind. "I don't have to knit my clothes. I love to. It has something to do with pride—and satisfaction."

They rode on for a while and the farther they went, the more Teddy enjoyed the ride. It was different from a single rider bike. She felt a loss of control, but was able to relax so much more. Well, she would not want to ride this way all the time, but sometimes it was fantastic.

"Ready to go back?" the captain yelled, and suited the

action to the suggestion. In a moment, they were headed back toward the ranches, rolling along at a fast clip.

It seemed to take much less time to return than it had to go, probably because they had learned how to handle the bike better. They stopped and got off the bike beside Brand's pickup.

"Thanks a lot," Teddy said. "That was really fun. Maybe we can do it again someday. May I ride with you to take it back?"

"Back?" Brand look at Teddy questioningly. "Oh, you thought I rented it? Teddy, this bike is ours—for romantic riding anytime, anywhere. Could we keep it in your garage?"

"Aren't you forgetting something?" The gravelly voice came from behind an overgrown shrub. Then Gram stepped out. "I'm ready for my try now. Who's riding with me?"

Brand smiled at the old lady. "Since I'm used to riding in front, and since you'll be in back no matter who goes, I think it'll be safer for you if I take you this first time. Okay?"

"Cut the talk and let's go." She climbed on the back seat and lacked six inches of reaching the pedals. Brand dropped the seat as low as it would go, and the two took off down the driveway.

Teddy watched with a dreamy smile on her face. She watched them all the way down the driveway and noticed they had turned in the same direction she and Brand had. She knew he would be extra careful with Gram, realizing how fragile her old bones had become. As she stood there thinking about Gram and Brand and what a lovely life she had before her, an old car turned into the driveway, and lumbered slowly toward her. She waited.

Finally, the car wheezed to a stop, amid a cloud of black

smoke from the exhaust system, and a woman, in her late forties, stepped out. "Is this the Marland ranch?"

Teddy glanced at the woman. She stood a little shorter than Teddy, and somewhat heavier. Her dark blonde hair, straggling to her shoulders, looked as though it had never been washed. Too much dark blue makeup surrounded pale blue eyes, and oversized glasses hid much of her face.

Her bright red lips opened to reveal darkly stained teeth. "Well, don't you know who owns this dump?" The woman practically spat the harsh words at Teddy.

Teddy nodded. "It's the Marland ranch."

The woman's pale eyes swept the yard and nearby area. "Well, where's the old lady?"

Teddy began to feel uneasy. This could be anyone. "She's not here right now. May I help you?"

The woman looked Teddy up and down. "Of course you can't help me. Get the old lady."

Teddy did not know whether to tell her that Gram would be back soon, or to get rid of her. She looked at the woman again, feeling as if she should know her. Maybe she had seen her somewhere before, but could not think where.

"If I can't help you, you may as well leave. I don't know exactly when she'll be back." Teddy tried to sound kind but businesslike.

"You ain't going to get rid of me that easy, you smart-mouthed kid. I'll wait." She turned to her old car, pulled the back door open, and a huge mutt jumped to the ground. It took one look at Teddy and then ran off.

"The dog can't be loose here," she said. "Call it quickly." The woman just glared at her. "Please! We have valuable animals." Still the woman did not move. Teddy turned and ran in the direction the dog had gone but could not find it. She looked for ten minutes. The dog was nowhere to be seen.

She returned to the woman, who sat on the rickety porch, smoking a cigarette. "Aren't you afraid the dog will get lost?" she asked. "This is a strange place for it, you know."

"I certainly do know this is a strange place. No doubt better than you. But as for the dog, I wish it would get lost, but that thing would come home if you dumped it in the middle of the ocean." She exhaled a breath of dark smoke, then watched it disperse, as though it were the most interesting thing she had ever seen.

A noise caught Teddy's attention and she saw Brand and Gram pedaling up the driveway. The woman saw it, too, and stood up to watch. They stopped and Gram hopped off and walked toward the porch and the women on it. Brand followed. Teddy could not believe how happy she was to see them.

Gram walked up the broken steps carefully, with Brand right behind. The woman stepped forward as Gram reached the top of the steps. They looked at each other, like two wary cats meeting for the first time. Teddy felt a horrible fear clutch her by the throat. Somehow, she knew this woman was bad news.

"Good afternoon," Brand said pleasantly. "May we help you with something?"

"Butt out, big boy. You don't belong here," the woman snarled. Her watery blue eyes never left Gram's face.

Brand tried again. "Pardon me, ma'am, but I do belong here. Could we do something for you?"

After a long, uncomfortable silence, Gram's lips moved. "Fritzi?" she whispered, almost inaudibly. A terrible choke came from Gram's throat as she tried to repeat her question. "Fritzi, is that you?"

thirteen

"Of course it's me, you old fool. Have your eyes gone bad like the rest of you? You look about a hundred and ten years old."

Brand stepped up and dropped a well-muscled arm over Gram's shoulders. "Look here, young lady, if you won't be civil you can leave right now. No one comes around here and insults Gram."

Gram put a hand on Brand's arm. "It's all right, sonny." She turned to the woman, Fritzi. "You don't look like any spring chicken, either, in case you haven't been near a mirror lately. Must have been living in the fast lane."

"Where's the kid, old woman?"

"Don't you dare ask me about the kid. Don't you ever ask me about the kid again. Do you understand?"

Immediately, Teddy knew who the woman was! The rickety porch floor seemed to move under her feet and she felt her knees give way—then nothing.

"Come on, baby, you're all right." The gravelly voice was one of the sweetest sounds Teddy had ever heard, even though it seemed far away. Teddy opened her eyes to find herself on the porch floor with Gram kneeling beside her, holding a cool cloth on her forehead. She raised her eyes to meet Brand's concerned look.

"I don't faint," she said trying to sit up. The porch began moving again, and she settled back down. "Never," she insisted as she lay quietly. Then she saw the woman, standing on the edge of the top step, looking around at the

117

ranch, a cigarette hanging loosely from her mouth. Teddy raised a hand and pointed to the woman, but no words came from her throat.

Gram nodded. "I'm sorry, kitten. I hoped this would never happen, but we'll be all right."

The woman wheeled around. "You hoped I'd never come back? Never see my own kid? So what did you do, give it away?"

Teddy sat up and clutched her throat. She tried to speak but could not get it out. "I'm your kid," she finally squawked in a strange voice. "I'm the kid you didn't even name."

Fritzi whirled around to face Teddy. "What? A big horse like you?" Her questioning eyes went to Gram. "My kid must be about twelve, isn't it? And I can't remember if it was a boy or girl. You'd better not have given it away and you'd better get it out here, old woman, or I'll have the law on you."

Struggling to her feet, Teddy moved to the love seat at the end of the porch. Her face felt wet and she discovered she was crying.

Gram's eyes looked steel hard as they met Fritzi's. She pointed to Teddy. "She was your kid, but only until she got outside your body. Then you couldn't shed both of us fast enough, could you? Walked out the hospital door, when you were so weak you could barely stand on your two feet. How do you think that made me feel, Fritzi? But you wouldn't understand a mother's love, would you? You wouldn't have any idea how it feels to be terrified for your child, week in, week out."

Fritzi grabbed Gram by the shoulders and started shaking her, but Brand snatched the offending hands and threw them against their owner. "I want you to get into the car and take off," he growled. "And don't come back."

"I'll bet you'd like that, wouldn't you, cave man? Well, I'm not going anywhere." She pointed at Gram. "That old woman is about to die and I'm here to take over the ranch."

Brand sucked in a big breath and so did Teddy, but Gram laid her head back and cackled with laughter.

Fritzi looked alarmed as Gram continued laughing. "What's the old woman laughing about? Is she senile?" she asked.

"You came home because you loved us so much you couldn't handle it anymore. Is that how it is, Fritzi? But you can't even bring yourself to call me anything more personal than 'old woman'. Well, not-so-young woman, I have news for you. This ranch is now worth well over a million dollars, including the livestock. What do you think of that?"

Fritzi's eyes grew round, and they swept over the pastures, the alfalfa fields, even the yard. "I'm going to sell it the minute you die. Hopefully that won't be too many days from now."

"What about your little girl?" Gram asked, a crafty look in her eye.

Fritzi's eye flicked past Teddy. *She still has not asked my name or how I have been all these years,* Teddy thought. *And worse than that, she does not care one thing about Gram. How could anyone grow up with Gram and not love her?*

"What about her?" Fritzi repeated.

"Wouldn't you want her to have at least part of it?" Gram's lips stretched in an imitation of a smile.

Fritzi looked at Teddy again, then back to her mother. "Old woman, you don't know anything, do you? Here's the way it works. When you die, I get it. When I die . . ." she groped for a name, then settled for, "she gets it. If there's anything left. But I plan to spend it all." She dropped her cigarette butt on the old porch floor and lit another.

Gram laughed heartily, almost as though she were enjoying herself now. "Well, not-so-young woman, don't spend it too fast. I told you the truth when I said this ranch is worth more than a million, but I forgot to mention that I don't own it anymore. I'm just fortunate enough to live here."

Fritzi sprang at Gram, her face twisted into a horrible sight. Once again Brand stopped her, stepping between. "You aren't going to hurt Gram," he said softly. "We love her very much and plan to keep her a long time. Now, why don't you leave?"

Fritzi turned on Brand and attacked him with insane rage. Before he could stop the woman, her long fingernails raked his face several times, leaving tiny rivulets of blood oozing down his cheeks. Then, long red streaks appeared on his bare arms. Brand pinned her arms to her sides, rendering her helpless before she could do any more damage. The more she struggled, the tighter he held her, until her face grew so red it looked as though it might explode.

"You...you...you, jackass!" she screamed. "You bought the ranch, didn't you? Where's the money? I want the money, and I want it now!" She jerked wildly for another minute, then relaxed, coughing and totally exhausted.

Brand turned to the older woman with a quiet smile. "Gram," he said pleasantly, "could you get some fingernail clippers, please?"

A moment later Gram reappeared with the requested item. Brand pulled Fritzi against him, her back to his chest. His arms held her so tightly his blood smeared over her dress. "Gram's going to trim those fingernails," he murmured, almost in a whisper. "If you want the ends of your fingers left intact, I suggest you hold still." He held one of Fritzi's hands to Gram. "Cut them close," he instructed.

Fritzi held her hands still and said nothing during the ten-minute procedure, but whimpered quietly the entire time. When Gram finished, everyone, including Fritzi, knew the fingernails would not scratch anyone for quite some time. "Will you behave if I turn you lose now?" Brand asked.

Fritzi nodded. He released her and she examined her hands. "They'll be so sore I won't be able to use them," she wailed.

Just then, llama cries, the sound of several dogs yapping, barking, and finally screaming, interrupted the confrontation on the porch. Brand tore past the hole in the steps with Teddy close behind. Gram came as fast as she could. They all temporarily forgot Fritzi, but she followed Gram as they all ran to the north pasture where the horrible sounds emanated from.

When Teddy arrived, she found Brutus and Caesar standing over Fritzi's badly chewed-up mutt. A three-year-old brown llama stood to one side, her head hanging, and blood running down her chest. Teddy pointed at the dog on the ground. "Keep it there!" she screamed to Brutus and Caesar, then turned to Brand. "Help," she whispered.

Brand moved to the llama's head and Teddy began searching for the source of the blood. She found a slash on each side of the llama's throat and shoved her hands against the wounds. But the blood flowed between her fingers. Almost immediately the llama dropped to her knees, then turned on her side and lay flat on the ground. Blood still flowed from the wounds, but slower. A moment later, the blood stopped and the llama's eyes opened with a glazed, unseeing appearance. Brand took Teddy into his arms and softly held her.

"I'm sorry, Teddy Bear. I'm so sorry." He bent his face

against hers and said nothing more, just continued holding
her tight. Teddy cried for several minutes, then took some
deep breaths. There were things to do here and she must get
hold of herself. The dog! Her dogs would still be watching
it but they must be relieved.

She lifted her bloody, tear-streaked face. "Thank you,
Brand. I'm all right, now." She turned to see Brutus and
Caesar, their fangs bared, standing over the other dog. Fritzi
stood watching, but Gram had disappeared. Teddy turned
back to Brand. "Where is she?" she asked.

He shook his head. Then Teddy followed Fritzi's eyes
toward the old log house. Gram hurried toward them,
holding a small rifle in her hands! The old lady looked at no
one and said nothing, but walked up to the dogs. She made
a sweeping motion with her right arm and spoke to the dogs.
Brutus and Caesar jumped to their feet and disappeared into
the herd of llamas that were standing around. Then Gram
shot the dog in the head, from a distance of about six inches.

"I'll call someone to take care of the carcasses," she said
calmly, then walked away toward the house.

Brand put his arm around Teddy again. "Are you ready to
go, love?"

Teddy walked to the llama, knelt beside it and petted its
back with both hands. She buried her face in the soft wool.
Then she stood to her feet, and held out her hand to Brand.
"I'm ready."

They walked slowly to the house, arm in arm. Fritzi
followed, several feet behind. When they reached the house,
Brand looked at the blood covering his arms and clothes, his
own, from Fritzi's attack, and the dead llama's. "I better go
shower and change. I can be back in twenty minutes."

Teddy nodded. "Yes, I'll do the same." Brand barely

touched her lips with his and then carefully ran down the steps. Teddy stepped inside and took off her shoes. She had nearly reached the hall door when she heard Fritzi clattering across the floor, and Gram appeared from the kitchen.

"Get those shoes off before you come into my house," Gram yelled, pointing at the front door.

Fritzi looked shocked, but backed up and stepped out of her scruffy pumps. Then Gram pointed to the utility room. "Now go wash the filth off you." Fritzi moved in the direction Gram indicated and Teddy ran for the shower.

Brand reappeared in less than thirty minutes looking clean and shampooed. The deep red lacerations in his face looked even angrier than before he left. He moved straight to Teddy. "Are you all right?" he asked tenderly.

Fritzi, rocking in the old wooden rocker, stopped suddenly. "What's this 'poor little Teddy' stuff? She only lost a silly looking animal, and she has a million others just like it. That old woman shot my dog right in front of my face. My pet, that went everywhere with me. And don't think she's going to get away with it. What's more, I'm positive those two white-eyed dogs of yours killed that . . . thing. When two dogs get together anything can happen. I read that in the paper. I'm going to call the Humane Society right away." She headed toward the telephone.

Gram stepped between Fritzi and the phone. "Shut up and sit down!" she growled. "Let me tell you something. If it hadn't been for those two white-eyed dogs of ours, we'd have lost many llamas, rather than just one. Let me tell you something else. Each and every llama is a personal pet of Teddy's. You saw how much she loved Cocoa, didn't you? Now, let me tell you this. That llama your dog killed was worth $20,000, maybe more, and she was due to have a baby in four months, which would have been worth a considerable amount too. One last thing. Ranchers around here take a very dim view of stock-killing dogs. No way, no way in this world could your dog have lived after what it did."

"Maybe you'd like to make some monetary restitution for the llama," Brand added quietly.

Fritzi, did not answer, but pulled out a cigarette. "Don't light it!" Gram's harsh voice instructed. "No one has ever smoked in this house and you aren't going to be the one to start."

Fritzi shoved the cigarette back into her purse and stood up, facing the group. "So, it's going to be three against one, is it? I didn't expect to be welcome here. Well, don't think I came back because I wanted to. I hated this place when I left, and it hasn't improved a bit. I only came back as a last resort, and I mean I tried everything else. I have a bad knee and can't stand on it to cook anymore. So I guess I'm stuck with you."

"That may well be," Gram said, "but I'm not sure we're stuck with you. You have absolutely no claims to our home, our food, our devotions, or our care. You forfeited that years ago, as well as all rights to Teddy."

"Tough, old woman. I don't have two dimes to rub together, and owe several thousand on charge cards, so what are you going to do, pitch me out in the street?"

She cast a quick glance at Brand. "I suppose you're the guy who bought the ranch, so you must have enough money to put up with me."

Gram shook her old head, but her eyes had a gleam. "I didn't sell the ranch, not-so-young woman. I gave it away several months ago. In fact, you're just six months too late."

Fritzi shook her head. "I'll admit you're dumb, old woman, but you aren't that dumb. You didn't give it away."

"Want to see the papers?" Gram got up and disappeared into her bedroom, returning a moment later with some stapled papers and tossed them to Fritzi.

After reading the papers a moment, Fritzi's face whitened. Her eyes met Teddy's. "She gave it to you? She gave this whole stinking place to you? For nothing?" She turned back to her mother. "How could you do this? She's only a granddaughter. I'll break this like a piece of cracked glass. I've heard about breaking wills before."

Gram smiled gently. "Isn't a will. I gave it to her. Well, technically, I sold it to her for one dollar. Just to be legal." Her eyes, filled with love, turned to Teddy. "Now, kitten, see why I insisted? It's all yours, safe and sound."

After Brand had left, Teddy made up a bed in the spare room for Fritzi and they all went to bed, feeling much exhausted from the highly charged emotions of the day, and with nothing settled as far as Fritzi was concerned. As Teddy tried to have her evening talk with her Lord she kept hearing bumps and thumps from Fritzi's room. How mad was she, anyway? Finally, Teddy told God goodnight and fell asleep.

The next morning, when Teddy went to feed the llamas, she found Brand already starting. "I thought I'd like to be with you this morning. I knew it would be hard, this first time after Cocoa . . . you know." She walked into his arms and he held her for a little while. The llamas watched and nudged them, eager for their breakfast. Suddenly, he pulled away and looked around. "Where is he?" he asked, as though frightened.

"Who? Oh, you mean Casanova. He's around some-where. Maybe he's getting used to you."

Brand started breaking apart bales of alfalfa hay and

dropping them behind the pickup. "He might be, but I don't feel like taking any chances." He worked a little while, then began chuckling.

"What could be so funny at half past five in the morning?"

"I just got to thinking. Wouldn't it be funny if Casanova spit on Fritzi?"

"I don't know. Brand, I'm sorry I never told you about my mother. Would you like to talk about it now?"

fourteen

He reached inside and shut off the motor, and they climbed onto the hay in the back of the pickup. "I want to know everything about you, my love." The baled hay jiggled when he pulled her close, but they managed to stay put.

"I never had a father. None at all. If Fritzi knew who he was she never told Gram. I've cried a lot of tears over being . . . illegitimate."

Brand kissed her soft brown hair. "Baby, why should you be so upset? You didn't do it."

Teddy snuggled close and continued talking as though she had not stopped. "Fritzi wanted an abortion in the worst way, but they weren't legal yet, and Gram hated the idea. So she had me, but when I was one day old, she ran away from the hospital, cleared out her and Gram's $3,000 checking account, stole Gram's almost-new car, and that's it. We never saw her again. I should say Gram didn't. Fritzi never saw me, even before she left. She refused." Teddy gulped. "And she didn't even remember whether I was a boy or girl. Or how old I was."

Brand rained kisses over her face. "How old was she when you were born, Teddy Bear?"

"Seventeen."

Brand nodded. "Pretty young. That isn't any excuse for what she did, though, to either you or Gram. Let's see, she's about thirty-eight now, then. I can't believe it. She looks fifty-eight."

Teddy nodded, holding Brand tightly. Then her head

flipped around. "Let's get out of here. Casanova's coming."

They jumped off the hay and started feeding the llamas. Casanova remained calm.

After they finished feeding, Teddy asked Brand if they could talk about him for a little while. They settled onto the tail gate of the pickup. "Okay," he said. "Am I in trouble?"

"No. But I've wondered about Celia. What really happened between you two. I thought I saw sparks."

He laughed. "So it worked! We thought it a dismal failure. Well, I met her on the riding trail as I said. But that's about where the story should have stopped. She's married and her husband was out of town. She asked me to take her to church so I told her about you and how I couldn't get to first base. So . . . we hatched up our little scheme to make you jealous." He held up his hand. "And don't get jealous now. The only thing we ever did was laugh and talk to each other when we knew you were watching. Otherwise, we're just friends."

Teddy heaved a sigh of relief. Now she could relax. For a fraction of a second the other problem—the one about the bank robbery in Eugene—tickled her mind, but she thrust it aside. She knew for sure that story did not have any more substance than the Brand and Celia one. She hurried in to breakfast with Brand, feeling clean and free. "How's the sore knee this morning?" she asked Fritzi.

"Well! I thought no one even heard that I had one. It's sore. It's always sore. I can walk but not much."

Brand wiped the last bite of his pancake in syrup and forked it into his mouth. "Gram, I hope you never forget how to make these fantastic pancakes," he said, then turned back to Fritzi. "I'm taking you to a doctor this morning."

"No, you aren't! I've been to plenty of doctors and they can't find the problem."

He nodded pleasantly. "We'll try one more." So, a little later, Brand took off toward Bend with Fritzi sitting unhappily beside him.

"What are we going to do with her, Gram?" Teddy asked after the car drove out of sight.

The old woman shook her head and Teddy thought she looked tired. "I don't know, kitten. We'd be within our rights to pitch her clothes out and lock the door, but I couldn't do that to anyone."

"What do you feel for her, Gram? Or would you rather not talk about it?"

Gram's eyes shot across the room to where Teddy sat. "How do I feel about my long lost daughter? I'm not sure. I may not feel anything. Then again, I may hate her a little for what she did to you . . . and me. And maybe, behind all these feelings, I still love her. I really don't know. Sometimes emotions are like that, you know. It takes a while to figure them out. Let's wait and see what the doctor says."

Brand and Fritzi came home an hour later with no news. "I paid the doctor and made Fritzi agree to ask him to talk to me," Brand said. "The X-rays showed nothing, there is no swelling or discoloration, but the doctor said there could be tenderness. He said knee problems are impossible to verify or disprove."

Fritzi looked triumphant. "So, old woman, are you going to throw me out?"

Gram looked grim. "Are you able to pull your own weight around here?"

"If I were, I wouldn't be here."

Gram looked at Teddy. "What do you say, Teddy?"

"I can't imagine turning out my own mother," Teddy said, smiling ruefully. "But then again, I can't imagine this person being my mother. It's up to you, Gram, she's a complete stranger to me."

"May I interrupt this family discussion?" Brand asked. "Why don't you not make any decision at all, but just take it one day at a time?"

"See here, you conceited jerk, you keep your big mouth out of family discussions." Fritzi reached in her pocket for a cigarette, then pulled it back empty.

"Wait a minute," Gram said. "Brand is very much a part of this family. Much more so than you, so don't expect him to be barred from anything that goes on around here."

"How does he get the privilege of calling himself a family member? What great thing did he do?"

"I'm marrying Teddy," Brand informed her. "And Gram, too, for that matter."

Fritzi pointed at Brand. "He's marrying her for the million," she yelled at Gram. "He couldn't want her. She's nothing but a kid. Don't you people have a brain in your head?"

Ignoring Fritzie's rude comments, Gram scrambled to her feet and stood over her. "Brand had a great idea. You can stay for now, but only if you get that rotten tongue under control. You gave up your place in our home and hearts many long years ago. If you stay now, you're nothing but a charity case, so sweeten up, or take off. Which will it be?"

"I have no choice. But neither do you. I'll stay and take whatever you barbarians dish out. I don't even have a dog to be on my side."

"Don't you ever mention that dog again!" Brand shouted. "You'll answer to me if you do!"

Fritzi got up and rushed to her room, closing the door with a crash.

"Let's hope she stays there," Gram said, smiling wryly.

Brand got to his feet. "I have work to do, but may I come over tonight?"

"Of course," Gram answered. "Plan to eat with us."

After Brand left, Teddy and Gram went outside and did their necessary work. When they stopped for lunch they did not see Fritzi. "Let's just keep real quiet," Gram whispered as they ate.

She appeared while Gram and Teddy cooked supper that night; she did not offer to help. Brand arrived for supper, and the meal was relatively pleasant. Fritzi kept quiet.

Brand helped do the dishes then took Gram aside. "Teddy and I'd like to go into Bend for a movie," he said quietly, "but we're wondering if you'll be all right alone with Fritzi."

"Sure. She won't bother me. You two go on and have a nice evening."

After the movie, Brand took Teddy to Pioneer Park, beside the Deschutes River. They walked hand in hand to the sparkling water, bubbling enthusiastically against the stone wall. The half moon dropped its silver beams on the quiet park, turning the lush, green grass to silver and the trees into large, dark shadows, moving gently in the small breeze. They sat at a picnic table beside the water and watched the moon playing hide and seek with fluffy white clouds.

"Are you warm enough?" Brand asked.

"Yes, but the nights are really getting cold. Pretty soon it will be freezing every night," Teddy said.

"I guess we'd better bring quilts next time we come. Well, my little Teddy Bear, have you thought any more about getting married? I'm not in favor of long engagements—especially ours."

She leaned her head on his shoulder. "I did for a while, but

Fritzi sort of blew everything else from my mind. Oh, Brand, what will we do with Fritzi when we get married?"

Brand turned Teddy in his arms. "You look like an angel with the moonlight bathing your face," he murmured. His lips dipped to hers and her arms found their way around his neck. She felt his hair and dug her fingers through it, as his lips fluttered against hers. He gave her one more quick hug and pulled away from her. "She isn't going to live in the same house with us, that's for sure."

"Who isn't going to do what?" Teddy asked, plummeting back to earth.

"Fritzi isn't going to live with us."

"What about Gram?"

"She's going to live with us."

"What if Gram has to take care of Fritzi?"

"No way, love. Fritzi isn't an invalid. She's going to have to figure something out. Something besides Gram's charity. Gram's quite a woman, but a little too old to start caring for a miscreant."

When Teddy walked into the old ranch house, Gram was busily sewing pink butterfly quilt pieces together and Fritzi was nowhere to be seen.

Gram motioned toward the bedrooms. "Watched a couple of programs and took off. Didn't say a word all night." Gram's eyes twinkled merrily. "She was a lot better company than I expected."

The next morning, as the three women ate breakfast, strange screeching noises brought them to the front porch. Brand had brought a small load of lumber on his pickup and, with a crowbar, he stood busily ripping the porch off the house.

"I do believe Superman has come to the rescue," Fritzi said.

Brand looked up and smiled, then got to his feet and kissed Teddy. "Good morning, Teddy Bear. I decided to repair my damage."

"We didn't fix your leg; you don't have to fix our house," Gram said.

"Oh, but I do. I'll probably be the guy who falls through the hole. This is your water day, Teddy, so I know you and Gram don't have time to help, but Fritzi, you're going to help me."

The frowzy woman looked down at her old polyester dress. "And what would I look like after I handled that mess?"

"We have a shower for that purpose," Gram answered. "And, while you're at it, please wash your hair. I have a hard time eating with that mess sitting at the table. Come on, Teddy." They walked a few feet, then Gram turned back to Brand. "How long's that job going to take, son?"

"Most of the day, I think." he answered. Then he grinned. "Not quite so long with Fritzi helping."

The gravelly voice answered immediately. "She'll help. Lunch will be served at noon . . . to everyone who spends the morning working. And supper at six o'clock likewise."

Teddy and Gram took off and spent the morning handling the irrigation. At noon they found the old steps gone and the new ones coming along. Fritzi had disappeared.

Brand shook his head when Gram asked if she had been helping. Fritzi did not put in an appearance at the lunch table. "How are we going to keep her out of the food while we're working?" Teddy asked.

"Easy. We're going to lock her out," Gram said.

Teddy gasped. "You wouldn't dare!"

"Oh yes she would. And I'll be the bouncer," Brand said, laughing out loud.

Gram knocked on Fritzi's door. "Come out of there and help Brand finish the steps."

No response.

"Go get her, Brand. I don't feel like begging."

"I'm coming in," he called, then opened the door, walked in, lifted Fritzi off the bed, and carried her to the front porch, kicking and screaming.

Gram locked the door and handed the key to Brand. "You may need to go in."

Later, when Gram and Teddy came, tired and dusty, to prepare supper, Brand was sitting on the top step. He stood and touched Teddy's lips with his, then he made a sweeping motion over the steps as his eyes met Gram's. "What do you think?"

"Better than when they were new," the grating old voice answered. "I especially like that rough stuff you put over the top. A person would have to work at slipping on them now."

Teddy looked around for Fritzi. "Where's your helper?"

Brand shook his head. "I haven't had a helper. As for that woman, I have no idea where she went."

Fritzi did not appear for supper but came in later, left her shoes at the door, and went to her room.

"Shampoo your hair and shower," Gram said as she passed by. But they did not hear the water run.

Teddy read her new llama magazine while Gram worked on her quilt. Brand had gone home to shower. "Hey, Gram, here's something that sounds interesting. An exotic animal sale, including llamas, in Macon, Missouri."

"Too far away."

"I know. I was just telling you about it."

"How much are the llamas?"

"It's an auction, Gram."

Brand walked in, removed his boots, washed his hands, and settled down beside Teddy. After kissing her hello, he removed one of her hands from the magazine and held it. "What's this about an auction?"

"Oh, I just saw it in this magazine. An exotic animal auction in Missouri. They're going to sell llamas."

He came to life in a hurry. "Hey, that would be fun. Do you want to buy more llamas?"

"No," Gram said. "We have our full herd."

"I wasn't thinking about buying," Teddy said. "I was wondering how much one of ours would bring at a national auction. We have some fantastic animals."

No one said anything, and Teddy started searching her mind for her best llama. One that had been born on the place. Her prettiest young female popped into her mind. Cocoa. She sat a moment, then ran to the bathroom and dropped to a sitting position on the edge of the bathtub. Putting her head in her hands, she let the tears run. After a while, she got herself under control and washed her face in cold water.

Gram walked through the open door while Teddy dried her swollen face. "It's Cocoa, isn't it?" she whispered.

Teddy nodded, keeping her face covered with the towel.

"She's the first one that came to my mind, too, but we have lots of beautiful llamas."

"Yeah," Brand added, from the bathroom doorway, "we can find plenty of good animals, and I'll go along and help you."

"Wait a minute," Gram said, as they walked back to the kitchen. "Who said we're taking anything to that auction?"

Brand shrugged. "Sorry. It sounded to me as though you were."

Teddy felt sorry she had ever mentioned the silly sale. "Of course we can't, but I was thinking of taking only one. We might lose our shirts at a place like that."

Brand turned on the TV and captured Teddy's hand. Gram worked on her quilt and Teddy half-watched the program, leaning on Brand's shoulder, while she read her magazine.

"If the sale were only a few hours' drive away, it would be different," Gram muttered, forty-five minutes later.

Teddy looked up and smiled. "I know, Gram. It's way too far."

After a while, Brand flipped off the TV. "I don't mean to be a trouble maker, Gram," he said, "but Fritzi hasn't eaten since breakfast. Do you still feel that she should do some work around here?"

"I sure do."

"Well, I think you fell on the only way to make her work. But how can we keep her out of the kitchen while you sleep?"

Gram's eyes flashed around the roomy old kitchen. "I doubt we could lock the refrigerator. And if we could, there's food in a lot of cabinets. I don't know." Her eyes turned to Teddy. "I'm a little too tired to take turns watching. What do you think, kitten?"

Teddy looked around. The only hope would be to lock Fritzi out of the house, which they could not do at night. Or could they lock the kitchen? She looked at the doorway into the living room. It was not very wide. Maybe they could block it. Then her eyes fell on the old door pushed against the wall. She had looked at it all her life until she did not even see it anymore. She jumped up, moved the chair away from the door, and closed it. "Voilà!" she cried triumphantly.

"Hey!" Gram said. "I'd forgotten all about that door. But how could we lock it?"

Brand examined the door and how it fit against the frame. As he looked it over, his eyes danced. "I'll bet I could rig up a lock on there."

In a little while he had it locked from the kitchen side. "But how are we going to get through?" Teddy asked.

"I'll lock it and go out the back door for tonight," Brand said. "In the morning you'll have to go out the front way and in the back door. Be sure not to lock the key in the kitchen. Tomorrow I'll get a hasp and padlock."

fifteen

When Teddy returned from her morning chores, she found Gram busy in the kitchen and Fritzi sitting on the front porch. "She's plenty mad," Gram said, stirring the oatmeal.

"I notice she isn't in here helping you, though."

"Nope. She hasn't come to that yet. Are we really going to let her wait to eat until she works?"

"I don't know, Gram. You have to be the judge. Do you know if she tried to get into the kitchen last night?"

"She sure did. Cussed me out royal for locking it."

"That wasn't very nice. What could she do today that wouldn't be too strenuous?" Teddy laughed.

Gram thought a moment. "How about the laundry? Surely loading three loads of clothes into the washer and dryer wouldn't be too much."

"Right. And let her fold the stuff, too."

Gram snapped her fingers. "Rats. If we let her into the utility room, she won't do the laundry, she'll get into the food."

Teddy shook her head. "You can stay inside and watch her. There isn't much to do outside right now. You can work on your quilt or make some applesauce."

"All right. Let's eat, then you can go tell her."

A little later, Teddy sat on the love seat beside Fritzi. She gave Fritzi a friendly smile. "Gram wondered if you'd do the laundry this morning? It's only three loads, plus whatever you have." It was the first time she was alone with Fritzi, and she felt a little nervous.

"What's with you, kid? Do you have a mind of your own? Or are you some kind of robot of the old woman's?"

"I think I have a mind of my own. Why do you doubt that?"

"I never heard of anyone starving their own mother to death."

"You aren't a mother to me, Fritzi. Gram's my mother. A fantastic one, too. She's been everything to me. Mother, father, grandmother. I couldn't have asked for more. But that's beside the point, isn't it? No one's trying to starve you. But don't you know, even the Bible says if you don't work you don't eat? We aren't asking you to work like Gram or me. Just a little to show some family spirit." She reached for Fritzi's hand, but the older woman jerked it away. Teddy stood up and smiled again. "Come on, what do you say, are you ready to join the family?"

"What can I say? I suppose I'll have to try, even if it puts me in the hospital."

"Great. And I promise we won't ask you to do too much. I'll see you at lunchtime."

As Teddy moved the llamas from the north pasture to the south that morning, she looked them over carefully. Which would she take if she did happen to go to that sale? She had a lot of fine animals, and it really would be exciting to see how they compared to other herds. When Teddy came in for lunch she found Fritzi lying on the couch in the kitchen, worn out, but the laundry had been done and put away.

Gram announced lunch and Fritzi staggered to her feet. "Where's lover boy?" she asked in a petulant voice. "Doesn't he eat all his meals here?"

"Not yet," Gram grated, "but soon."

Fritzi barely waited for Gram's "Amen" to snatch a sandwich, which she stuffed into her mouth before she tasted her soup. "Yeah, when is this big wedding coming off?" She drank her milk in one long gulp, then broke a handful of crackers into her soup.

"We haven't set a date," Teddy said.

"You messed up their plans," Gram added.

Everyone ate quietly for a few minutes, until Fritzi dropped her soup spoon onto the table with a clatter. "I'm ready for dessert, old woman," she announced.

"Is that right? Well, just get yourself an apple from the refrigerator," Gram said.

"Forget the apple," Fritzi snarled, walking out of the room.

Gram looked at Teddy, the corners of her mouth jerking up and down. "I'm not sure she has the family spirit down pat yet."

Teddy laughed, walked around the table, and hugged Gram. "I hope you aren't letting her get to you. Just remember, you're the best."

Gram's eyes misted. "Thanks, kitten. I needed that. Now, what are we going to find for our fine guest to do this afternoon?"

"More? Today?"

"Of course, more. Are you quitting for the day? Am I?"

"No, but—"

"Do you trust her to iron your clothes?"

"Sure. I don't have anything that great."

But when Teddy came in after the evening feeding, she found Gram alone in the kitchen. "Her royal highness refused to work," she told Teddy. "I'm predicting she won't work unless she's on the brink of starvation."

Teddy and Gram ate alone before Brand called to say he would be over, but it would be late.

Teddy hauled out her knitting and turned on the television, disappointed that Brand was not with her. She could not believe how much she missed him.

Fritzi joined them in the kitchen and watched the programs, too. "Is TV the most exciting thing you ever do around here?" she asked Teddy.

"We do lots of exciting things," Teddy said. "Remember the day you came? Brand had just brought a tandem bike over and we all learned to ride it."

"Yahoo," Fritzi said in a monotone. "I hope I never have to do anything that exciting. It might cause a heart attack."

"Well, it was fun to us," Teddy insisted.

A light tap on the front door interrupted the conversation. Sighing, Teddy went to the door. She had recognized the tap and threw open the door, less than eager to face Lynden. He stood on the porch, all smiles, looking even thinner and paler than she remembered.

She forced a smile to her lips. "Well, Lynden, what a nice surprise. I'm glad to see you've forgiven us for . . . whatever we did." She opened the door and he stepped in, dropped his shoes, and made for the bathroom to wash his hands. When he returned, she led him into the kitchen.

"Fritzi," she said, hesitantly, "I'd like for you to meet our good friend, Lynden Greeley." She held her hand toward Fritzi. "Lynden, Fritzi."

Lynden greeted Gram and sat down beside Teddy on the couch.

"Who is she?" he quietly asked Teddy.

"Oh, didn't we tell you?" Fritzi gushed. "I'm Teddy's mother. Yes, she's my little girl."

Lynden sat still a moment, attempting to watch television, then turned to Fritzi. "Her mother? I didn't know she had a mother. Where have you been all these years?"

Fritzi bowed her head sadly. "We've been separated." She raised her head and smiled victoriously. "But we found each other again several days ago, and we're all so happy we just don't know what to do."

"Wow, a reunion! I know what to do. I'm going to write a story about it for the paper!" He rose off the couch in his excitement.

"You aren't writing anything," Gram snapped.

He settled back down like a balloon going flat. "Come on, Nelle, don't say that. This sounds like my big chance."

"It may sound like it, but believe me, it isn't. Forget it." Gram's coarse voice sounded as though she meant business.

If Gram had slapped his face, he would not have looked more injured. Fritzi moved from the rocker to the couch and hooked an arm through his. "Come out to the porch and I'll tell you all about it, Lynny. The old woman's just too shy, but she really wants you to know."

She tugged on his arm and he stood up, looking considerably happier. They started out the kitchen door into the living room.

"Freeze!"

They both stopped in their tracks. "Lynden," Gram said, "I know you're upset with Teddy, but I also think you care for her and wouldn't hurt her. Well, take my word for it, if you put one word about this in the paper you'll hurt her so badly she'll never recover."

Lynden's gray eyes searched out Teddy's. "Is that right?"

Teddy nodded. "It has no place in the paper. I don't know what Fritzi would tell you, but it's a sad, rotten story. Please don't."

He hesitated. "Maybe I'll just listen to it."

"Let her tell it in here then," Gram said.

Lynden nodded and settled onto the couch beside Teddy. "Great with me."

Fritzi did not return, but headed for the hall. "Let them tell you then, turkey," she spat at Lynden before she disappeared.

Lynden turned expectantly to Teddy. "Okay, I'm all ears."

Gram sighed and leaned back in her chair. "I'll tell him. It's an ugly story, Lynden, and you agree this is off the record, right? It's also a short story. Fritzi ran off right after Teddy was born and we didn't see or hear from her again until she appeared on the place a few days ago."

Lynden's face turned a shade whiter. He sat quietly a few moments, thinking about what he had heard. Then he turned to Teddy. "How awful! Somehow I supposed your mother was dead. What about your father?"

Teddy shook her head.

"Oh. I'm sorry, Teddy. I really am sorry, and I wouldn't think of printing that." He reached for her hand and brought it into his lap. A moment later, he lifted it into his view. "What do I feel on—" He stopped when he saw the dainty ring with the large diamond reflecting the kitchen lights. "When did all this happen?"

"About a week ago," Teddy said. She could not keep the happy smile away from her face.

"I told you not to do this," Lynden said. "You know the guy's nothing but trouble waiting to happen, don't you?"

"She found out he's not the man," Gram volunteered. She had her quilt piece in her lap again, sewing the butterfly to the bright background.

"What did she do, ask him?" he asked sarcastically.

"Don't worry how she did it," Gram advised, quietly.

"Just be thankful she's not marrying trouble."

"Teddy," Lynden cried, "you've been misinformed. I know he's the man. Positively. More news has come into the office and it all points to Brandon Sinclair. It leaves no doubt in my mind that he's the bank robber. None at all. He'll have a nice long prison sentence to face when he's caught. And I'm going to make sure he's caught." He got up and marched straight to the front door, stiff as an overstarched shirt.

Teddy heaved a sigh, but followed him. "Why do I feel like I'm living through a rerun, Lynden?"

He pulled on his second shoe and turned the doorknob. "I'd like to wish you happiness, Teddy, but wishes don't come true when you purposely go against what you know to be right." He shut the door and Teddy threw the dead bolt.

"Gram, isn't it time we had a little tranquility in our lives?" she asked, picking up her knitting.

Gram put her work down and got up. "I was just thinking that. Want some coffee?"

The front door nearly crumbled beneath the next attack and Teddy jumped to her feet. "Make some for Brand too, Gram. I'm ashamed to say I forgot all about him for a few minutes."

Gram waved Teddy toward the front door. "Go get him. I want to talk to you both."

"Sorry to be so late," he said, kissing her. Then he clasped her to him. "Just hold me a minute, love."

Teddy looked at his ashen face. "What's happened, Brand?"

"Is it that visible? Well, I don't want you to get upset, and it really isn't all that terrible. I'm just not very tough. We just lost a calf. The mother's going to be fine with a few days' good care, and the calf wasn't worth a whole lot of money.

I just feel bad about the loss of life." He shook his head. "It tried so hard to live." He gave Teddy another squeeze and she felt him swallow hard. "And we tried really hard to help it live. The vet said it just wasn't meant to be."

"Sit down and have a cup of coffee," Gram said. "I want to talk to you two. Maybe it'll help for you to think about something else."

Brand and Teddy settled onto the couch, she in the circle of his arm. "You don't know how good you feel, Teddy Bear," he said, kissing her cheek.

Gram set the coffees on the low table and put a plate of oatmeal cookies between them. "How would you two like to take a couple of llamas to the sale in Missouri?" she asked.

"I'd love it!" Brand said without hesitation. "Teddy, get your magazine."

"Just a minute," Gram held up a hand and Teddy settled back down beside Brand. Then Gram spoke to Brand as though Teddy were not there. "You've seen what came home to roost, haven't you, son?"

He nodded.

"Well, you understand that things like that could make an old woman a little crazy, but I have to say this, crazy or no. I'll be happy for you two to make the trip, but only after you promise me that my girl will come home as innocent as she leaves. I love her far more than my own life and I couldn't bear for anything to hurt her."

"I love her more than my own life too," he said. "I'd never hurt her, Gram, even her reputation, so why don't we all go? Let Fritzi take care of the place." He stood and kissed the wrinkled cheek. "Let's make it a vacation. I'll bet it's been a while since you've had one."

Teddy laughed, pulled Brand to the couch, and handed

him his coffee. "I agree with Brand, Gram. Please won't you go with us? You'd get so excited at the auction I'd have to hold you down."

Gram shook her head. "Somebody has to mind the store, you know."

"I'll send Rolf over," Brand said. "Our work is slowing down a lot, now."

"What about Fritzi?" Gram asked.

"Let her take care of herself," Brand said. "We know for sure she's able to do that much."

Gram's eyes beamed with joy. "Well, I'll think about it. I'm just not sure we can both leave. But you can't believe how happy I am that you asked. Now, I'm going to bed and leave you two alone."

Brand pulled a hasp and padlock from his pocket. "No need, Gram, we aren't going to sit and spoon. I'm going to fix this door."

She went to bed anyway and Brand had the lock all screwed on in ten minutes. "Let's go sit on the porch and see if we can see the moon," Brand suggested.

They settled onto the love seat. "I don't see the moon," Teddy said, "but I see a fantastic trip in our near future. I'm already getting excited. I wonder, what llamas I should take?"

sixteen

Pandemonium broke loose in the form of cheering, foot stomping, whistling, and laughing. The crowd rejoiced with Teddy and she felt so weak she could not even move. Brand leaned down to her, his eyes laughing. "You don't believe it, do you, Teddy Bear? Do you still want to watch the camels, ostriches, and other stuff sold? Or do you want to leave?"

Suddenly, Teddy felt adrenalin pumping through her and she wanted to jump up and down. "I want to watch the others being sold, but I can't sit still."

"Let's get out of here for a while then. Maybe we'll come back later."

As they walked out, the loudspeaker crackled. "There they go, folks, the proud owners of the Marland llamas. We'll break for lunch now and, at half-past one, we'll start with the llama's large relative, the camel. See you in an hour and a half."

Teddy, Gram, and Brand were mobbed before they got to the pickup. Many in the crowd just wanted to congratulate them, but several inquired about buying llamas. Teddy gave them each her card with her address and phone number.

Finally, they sat in the truck and looked at each other in shock. "Duska just made you famous," Brand said. "Your llamas will always bring good money now." He rubbed his forehead with the heel of his hand. "And I hardly believed you when you said you could sell a female for $10,000."

Someone tapped on the window so Brand rolled it down. A big burly man thrust his hand in and shook hands with all three of them. "Fantastic," he said. "I'm really pleased with what this did for the llama industry, but your llama would have probably brought more at the Hart sale. They sell only llamas and all the llama breeders go there."

"We're just happy with the price we got," Brand said, unable to stop smiling.

"Right. I don't blame you, and the llama people will be more serious about this auction from now on, too."

The man walked away and Brand wasted no time getting the pickup on the highway. "Hungry?" he asked.

"No. Yes. I'm too excited to know. But we'll have to go back and tell the llamas goodbye pretty soon."

Brand turned to Gram. "You haven't said a word, young lady. What do you think? Are you too surprised to speak? Are you disappointed?"

Gram smiled then laughed out loud. "I'm just pretending I'm not here. That way I can enjoy the two of you a lot." She quieted for moment. "Yes, I guess I'm too surprised to talk. Wait until Fritzi hears."

They stopped at a restaurant to eat, but Teddy could not push the food down. She knew what had happened, but just could not believe it.

"Want to call Fritzi, Gram?" Brand asked as they walked out and past a telephone.

Gram shook her yellow-white hair wildly. "I want to see her face when I tell her. I don't think she believed we could ever get $20,000."

They went back to the auction and told Duska and Playboy goodbye, but Teddy could not sit down to watch the other sales. "I know I'll be sorry. How many times in my life am I going to see zebras and cougars auctioned off? But I can't help it, I want to go home."

Brand nodded understandingly. "I don't blame you, love."

They collected their bank-guaranteed check for the price of the two llamas, plus the thousand dollars from Lolli's auction market, minus ten percent for the auction fees. They walked away from Lolli's with a check for $75,150 tucked into the corner of Teddy's purse. When they reached the truck, she handed the check to Gram. "I'd feel a lot better if you held onto this," she said. "You know how I keep losing things."

"Let's head for home," Brand said after Gram had deposited the check into the most secret pocket in her purse.

They left in the early afternoon and hashed and rehashed the sale, laughing like happy children. After a tiny silence, Teddy uttered a long sigh.

"Are you okay, Teddy Bear?"

"Yes, but it just hit me that I'll never see Playboy or Duska again. But don't you agree they got good homes?"

"You bet! If I paid a fraction of that for an animal, I'd keep it in the house on a pillow. Teddy Bear . . . $65,000 for one animal?" And that launched yet another rehash of the sale, telling each other how much prettier their llamas were than the others.

Finally, the sun crept low in the western sky, then disappeared, pulling the daylight behind it. "I think I'm hungry," Teddy announced sometime later.

"Shall we stop for the night?" Brand asked. "Or should we eat and drive on? I could easily drive a few more hours."

After eating and then driving on for a few more hours, they finally stopped at a motel after midnight. "We're making good time," Brand said. "It's late and we're all exhausted, but we'll be home sooner than we expected." He kissed both Teddy and Gram good night and went to his own room. Teddy dropped into bed and fell asleep thanking God for answering the prayer she did not pray . . . and answering it more abundantly than she could have ever dreamed.

The next morning, Brand awakened them before six o'clock and they drove three hours before stopping for breakfast. Then, on again. That night, as the sun disappeared from view, Teddy asked to stop for the night. "Let's go out for a nice supper."

Gram decided to rest in the room and order some food from room service. Teddy had not come down from her cloud since the sale so she and Brand walked into the restaurant giggling together. They both enjoyed the perfectly prepared steak, salad, and french fries, followed by an out-of-this-world chocolate mousse. Then, they walked around, under a moon that looked round and orange.

A three-wheeled bike pulling a small carriage pulled up beside them on the quiet street. "You guys like a ride in the park?" the driver asked.

Brand looked down at Teddy, who nodded eagerly. He helped her in and they snuggled together as the man pedaled slowly along.

"Our life together reads like a storybook," Brand said, holding her close.

"Yes, rich, famous, and happy," Teddy giggled. "With fourteen children."

Brand jerked as though shocked. "What's the matter?" Teddy murmured. "Did I say the wrong thing?"

Then he laughed. "How many children? How about four or six? But fourteen?"

Teddy pulled him close and forgot all about children. In fact she forgot everything in the world except Brand and her. Then, "This is the end of the line. Hey, buddy, we're back where we started."

Brand helped Teddy down. He silently paid the man, who rode away on his contraption muttering, "... didn't even see the park."

They both burst out laughing and raced back to the motel. "The poor guy was right," Brand said, "we saw only each other."

Teddy pulled his head down for a quick kiss. "What else is there?" she asked quietly.

They pulled into the old ranch at midnight the next night. Gram ran up the new steps and unlocked the door. They all tumbled inside, each as glad to be home as the others. They went into the kitchen where Fritzi sat on the couch. Brand winked at Teddy. "Yeah, Playboy really shocked us. He brought $17,500."

"Wow!" Fritzi said. "That sounds pretty good if you're telling the truth. But you took a female, too, didn't you? Didn't she sell?"

Gram looked at Teddy who looked at Brand. He put on a sad look. "Yeah, she sold, but she only brought . . ." He looked mournfully at Teddy, as though he couldn't say it.

"$65,000!" Teddy screamed.

Fritzi jumped out of her chair. Then she dropped back down. "No way. You're just saying that to make me feel bad about Cocoa. I know what you're doing."

Gram did not say a word nor change expression. Teddy laughed happily. "She did, Fritzi. That Duska is one fine lady. But we have lots more like her."

"Know what we're going to do as soon as possible?" Brand asked.

"Get married, I suppose," Fritzi said, sarcastically.

Brand turned sincere eyes on Fritzi. "We were almost too busy to think about a wedding but once in a while the subject cropped up. We remembered we love each other though. Do you remember how it feels to be in love?"

Teddy walked out with Brand and left the two women snarling at each other like stray cats. "It almost seems as though we shouldn't be parted anymore, after the last week," she told Brand.

He kissed her gently and climbed into the pickup. "Thanksgiving can't get here quickly enough for me," he said. He tweaked her fingers that lay on the pickup door and drove away in the dark.

In the days that followed, Teddy and Brand worked hard and played hard. Every day of work and play brought them closer together, leaving not an inch of room for doubt of the rightness of their love.

Fritzi not only shampooed her hair but began fixing herself pretty and acting pleasantly. She cooked gourmet meals several times a week and always invited Brand to share them. One evening at supper, Fritzi turned her prettiest smile on Brand. "When are you going to teach me to ride?" she asked.

Brand's golden eyebrows shot into his forehead. "I wasn't aware that you wanted to learn."

"Of course I do. I'm only human and you always take the old woman. Why can't I go?"

"I'm not sure you could ride Pharaoh," he said thoughtfully. "He's pretty spirited."

"Ha! Surely you don't think the old woman can ride something I can't."

"That's exactly what I think."

"Let me ride Misty. The kid doesn't have to go all the

time."

"It's all right," Teddy said, "she can ride Misty."

"Misty's your horse, Teddy Bear, and no one except you is going to ever ride her again. Got it?" He snatched Teddy's hand, pulled it to his lips, kissed it, then returned it gently to her lap.

The next evening, Brand rode over on Thunder, leading three horses. "Who's that?" Teddy asked, pointing to a beautiful gray mare with dark spots on her back quarters. Her mane, tail, and feet were dark, too.

Brand shrugged, grinning as though embarrassed. "I picked her up today. Been looking at her for a while, but couldn't justify buying her. What do you think?"

Teddy took the kind head in her arms. "She's a gorgeous animal, Brand. What's her name?"

"Dove. She's an Appaloosa. I don't know whether she's gray like a dove or harmless as a dove. Either fits. She's a nice animal. But no race horse."

Teddy continued to pet Dove. "Hey. You bought Dove for Fritzi, didn't you?"

"For Fritzi to ride sometimes." He raised his eyebrows. "Great for a kid, too. She's a beginner's horse."

They rode after supper and Fritzi managed to stay on Dove's back. "You really should ride beside me, Brand," she whined. "I might need you if the horse bolts."

Brand grinned and stayed with Teddy. "She's not going anywhere. You can just be thankful if she keeps up with the rest."

"Pharaoh isn't happy with this stroll," Gram said. "We're going for a little ride." She gave the large horse his head and disappeared around a bend in the path.

"The old woman's going to kill herself," Fritzi mused.

"But then I guess you'd like that. All those llamas would really be yours then."

"You be quiet!" Teddy yelled. "The llamas are already mine, as well as the ranch. You saw the papers, so just be quiet. I love Gram and can't imagine living without her."

Fritzi shook her head and flitted a silvery laugh toward Brand. "Tsk, tsk. Quite a little fireball, isn't she? Doesn't take much to set her off."

seventeen

One evening after supper, Fritzi went into her bedroom and returned freshly made up and combed. She had even put on a fresh dress. "I was just wondering, Brand, honey, I need to run into Bend this evening for a minute. Could you do the honors?"

Gram sighed, dumped her quilt on the coffee table, and got up. "I'll take you. Let's go."

Fritzi casted an angry glance at Gram. "Sit down and work on your quilt, old woman. You're too old to be running around at night." She put the frown away and brought out a pretty smile. "How about it, Brand?"

Brand looked at Teddy. "I don't see why not. We haven't anything planned for the evening. What do you say, Teddy Bear?"

"Sure, we can find something to do while Fritzi does her business."

Fritzi's smile disappeared and the scowl covered her face again. "You may as well stay and check the llamas or something," she said.

Brand reached for Teddy. "Where I go, Teddy goes."

The smile came back. "I don't want her to come, Brand. Don't make me tell you why."

"You'd better, because if she doesn't go, I don't." Brand's placid look was gradually tensing up.

"All right, if I have to." Fritzi pulled Brand away from Teddy and stood on her tiptoes to whisper something into his ear. When he heard what she said, Brand relaxed and his eyes

155

brightened. "Oh. Okay, Fritzi, I understand, but couldn't Gram take you tomorrow?"

Fritzi made another pretty face. "I ask you, how much help would the old woman be?"

Finally, with a little more begging, Brand and Fritzi drove off toward Bend. "I wonder what she said to soften him," Teddy mused aloud.

"I don't know, but I don't like it. That woman is not good news. We'll have to watch her." Gram bit off a thread and spit it halfway across the room.

The two returned a few hours later, Fritzi in a fantastic mood, and Brand snapping at everyone.

"Was your trip successful?" Gram asked.

"Well, not exactly," Fritzi giggled. "But we sure had fun. We ran all over the malls until Brand was thirsty, so we stopped for some ice cream treats." She turned to Teddy and actually smiled at her. "Gotta admit, kid, you got good taste in men."

Brand had long since replaced Lynden as Gram and Teddy's escort to church. The first week, Fritzi had almost agreed to go, but backed out when she saw Gram's Sunday clothes. "Why should I go and be embarrassed by an old woman who's too senile to know she's in church?" was her excuse for staying at home.

But one Sunday morning she came from her bedroom with a yellow and black dress, deep blue eyelids, and a red mouth. She pranced out and danced toward Brand. "I decided I was being a bad girl, staying away from church just because of the old woman. Everyone knows she's crazy, so I guess it won't hurt me to go."

Gram jumped off the couch where she had been waiting

for Teddy. "Well, I'm embarrassed to go with a clown. You can count me out." She took off her straw hat and headed for her bedroom.

Teddy and Brand shook their heads and laughed. "They don't get along any better than they did when she was seventeen," Teddy said.

"And now you can see why, can't you?" Fritzi asked, giggling. "The old woman never could stand me. Jealous, I suppose. You know she was forty years old when I was born. That's older than I am now." She made an exaggerated shudder. "I just can't imagine having a baby now."

"You couldn't imagine having a child when you were younger either, the way I hear it," Brand said in a gentle voice.

"Hear, hear!" Teddy said, happy to hear him standing up to Fritzi. Teddy, also embarrassed by Fritzi's outlandish makeup, felt like following Gram's lead, but did not because of Brand. It was not his fault he got into this mess.

In church, Brand sat between Teddy and Fritzi and Teddy noticed that Fritzi crowded him more than she did. So she moved a little farther away; she did not want to do anything like Fritzi.

On the fourth day of November it dumped fifteen inches of snow in six hours. Teddy and Brand helped each other fix the loafing sheds to make the livestock comfortable, with hay and water handy.

That night Brand called and said he would be over later and for Teddy to be ready for some fun. She could not wait. She barely ate any supper and the clock hands crept around slowly. At half past seven, the familiar attack on the front door brought Teddy to her feet. Fritzi beat her to the door, though barely.

Brand stepped inside, covered with snow. "Get some warm clothes on, Teddy," he instructed, after lifting her to his frosty kiss. "We're going for a ride."

"How about poor wittow me?" Fritzi asked, talking baby talk directly into Brand's face. "I never get to do anything fun. Don't I get to go with you?"

"Sorry. The rig is only a two-seater. Hurry, Teddy, I'm getting too hot in here," he called.

"I bet that's because of little old me, don't you think?" She winked at him as Teddy arrived, dressed in a warm snowsuit with the hood pulled over her head and tied securely.

"I'm ready, Brand, and I feel like a snowman." She put on the boots she had carried to the door and they stepped out into the wintry world.

"Gram! Look what we're going to ride in." Thunder, Brand's huge stallion, wearing a dark blanket, stood hitched to a small red sleigh. Fit for a snow queen, the sleigh was low in front, the sides rising toward the back, with lots of fancy squiggles and curls all around. Thunder wore a gala red harness edged with small bells. When the large horse moved, the bells filled the night with their music.

Brand helped Teddy inside and tucked the heavy woolen blanket around them. "This is fantastic, Brand. I've never ridden in a sleigh."

Brand gave her a toothy smile and began singing "Jingle Bells." His clear baritone voice rang out through the first verse and chorus. Then he stopped and looked at Teddy. "Do you know the second verse?"

"Yes, shall we sing it together?" And they did, harmonizing through the second verse and chorus, the harness bells accenting the song.

After they finished, Teddy relaxed in the curve of his arm. "I love you for this," she said. "You couldn't have done anything more romantic."

Brand leaned across all their blankets and heavy clothing to kiss her. "I love you," he whispered.

They talked about the future as Thunder pulled them through the still night. Whether they should run both cattle and llamas or change entirely to llamas, whether they should live in Gram's house and run her farm and get someone to help Rolf with the other.

"I can't believe how still the night is," Teddy said. "Only Thunder's bells. Thank you, Brand, I love it. And I love you . . . so very much."

"In that case, it was worth all the trouble, my love."

"Was it a lot of trouble?"

"Sure was." His twinkling eyes contradicted his statement. "I had to take Thunder out behind that back shed and hook it up." He held her close and rearranged the wool blanket over them. "You see, I bought the sleigh several weeks ago, and I've been waiting impatiently for the snow."

"You mean the sleigh is yours?"

"Ours."

"Then we can go again?"

"Anytime you want. Are you ready to go home yet, Teddy Bear?"

"Yes, and it's been the greatest night of my life. Thanks again, my love."

Thunder realized he was on his way home and broke into a smooth canter several times.

When Brand walked Teddy to the house, they discovered Fritzi sitting outside in the love seat waiting for them. "My turn," she sang out.

"No way," Brand growled. "It's too late."

"Come on, you know you want one more little spin." She put both hands around his upper arm. "Please? I'd really like it."

Brand moved away from Fritzi. Her hands dropped to her side. "I'm tired and Thunder's getting cold," Brand said. "Maybe Teddy can take you for a ride tomorrow."

Fritzi threw her head prettily. "But it won't be the same." She swept her hand over the snow-covered vista. "If that isn't a story book scene I've never seen one. Please take me tonight."

Teddy stood on her toes and kissed his lips. "Why don't you take her for a little ride?" she whispered. "Just down to your driveway? I'm afraid her life has been pretty bleak."

"No!"

"Just for me?" she whispered again, their lips still touching.

He spun away, angrily. "Come on, Fritzi, but it's going to be short." Nevertheless, he helped Fritzi into the sleigh, and carefully tucked the robes around her.

Teddy went into the house and removed her snowsuit and sweater. Gram sat in the rocker, sewing finished quilt blocks together. "Where are the others?" she asked.

"Brand took Fritzi for a sleigh ride. Gram, he's so wonderful. He really didn't want to but after I badgered him into it, I noticed he covered her up so very gently and carefully."

"Hmph."

Teddy laughed. "What in the world does that mean, Gram?"

"It means she didn't need a sleigh ride."

"Oh, Gram, that's not like you. It's not like Brand either, but she sounded so pitiful I felt sorry for her."

"You should have left him alone," Gram finally grumbled.

"Gram," Teddy said, "that's not the way you taught me. You've always said it never hurts to go the extra mile for anyone—no matter whom."

"Humph! Well, I'm not saying it right now. I meant someone who needed help, not someone who wanted to tear up other people's lives." Gram's fingers slowed for exactly the amount of time it took her to say the ugly words, then began pushing the needle in and out again, with the speed of a bird picking up seeds.

Teddy picked up her knitting. She probably would not get anything done, but she hated to waste time. She worked fast and finished three rows, then held it up. "See, Gram, isn't it pretty?" She held a red piece of fuzzy rib knitting, the beginnings of a skirt to match the sweater she had just finished.

"Why don't you go on to bed, Gram?" Teddy asked fifteen minutes later. "I'll wait up to let Fritzi in."

"I'll wait with you."

After nearly a half hour, Teddy began to feel uneasy. "They couldn't have had an accident, could they, Gram? After all, what can happen in a sleigh?"

Finally, Gram grinned. "They could have gotten into a snow drift and got caught."

Then Teddy remembered her own sleigh ride. "Gram, Brand sang 'Jingle Bells' to me while Thunder's harness bells jingled in the still night. It was so beautiful. And romantic." Her knitting needles stopped as she remembered how glorious it was. "Gram, did you ever go sleigh riding?"

Gram's needle did not stop. A bright pink border began to appear around the butterfly. "Sure did, kitten."

"With Gramp?"

Gram's throaty laugh filled the room. "Don't ask. No, it was before I met your grandfather." They talked a while and somehow got around to the subject of Fritzi's leaving right after Teddy was born.

"Poor Gram. I've thought about how awful you must have felt to be saddled with a baby after you had raised your own and I've thought about how you must have worried about Fritzi. Was it awful? What did you tell people?"

Gram's eyes, looking all soft, turned to Teddy. "You've been the second biggest blessing, close behind your grandfather, of a large assortment of blessings that God's seen fit to shower on me, Teddy. Don't worry about that for a minute. What did I tell people? For a while I hedged, trying to protect Fritzi because I was certain she'd come back. But after a while I simply told people I didn't know where she was and that you were legally mine. That was the truth, you know. After a certain time, I forget now how long you have to wait, I got legal custody of you."

The front door slamming interrupted their talk and they both ran to the living room.

Fritzi stood by the door, looking as though she had been on a ten-mile hike. Her hair and even her eyelashes had turned white. Her shoulders also had more than a snowy cape over them. Teddy also noticed packed snow on both sides of her mittens. As her eyes took in the entire picture, she saw a lot of packed snow on Fritzi's knees. Knees that had only nylons between them and the snow.

"Well," Gram said almost jovially, "looks like you crawled home on your hands and knees." She laughed as though pleased about the whole thing.

"Why are you laughing, old woman?" Fritzi asked. "That Dr. Jekyll and Mr. Hyde that Teddy wants to marry is crazy.

First he sang 'Jingle Bells' to me right in time with Thunder's harness bells. When he finished the song, he just picked me up, laughing like a maniac, and dumped me overboard— several miles from here. Then, he told that big horse to run home fast. I heard him. And the horse took off as though the devil himself was chasing him. He probably knows how daft the man is."

eighteen

Teddy was shocked at what she had just heard. Never had she seen any trace of emotional instability in Brand. But she felt almost worse about something else—Brand had sung to Fritzi! Part of the thrill of the night had been that he had sung that song for her . . . just for her. And then he had sung it for Fritzi! Well, she had forced him into taking Fritzi for a ride.

Then she heard a big gravelly snort. "Bosh! Who do you think you're kidding?"

Of course it was not true. Fritzi just made it up. Teddy's eyes lifted to the older woman. She had to believe that Fritzi had just walked in the snow. Teddy's heart beat fast and hard. "Where's Brand now?" she whispered. Fritzi did not hear so Teddy swallowed hard and repeated the question.

"I don't know," Fritzi answered in a hard voice. "Probably whipping his horse into a lather somewhere trying to make it go faster."

Gram stood straight as a poplar tree. "Be quiet!" she demanded. "Teddy!" Teddy jumped to the harsh sound and looked down at Gram, who still stood stiff as old bread. "Don't you dare believe her. Don't you dare!"

"I want to hear her story once more," she told Gram. "Tell us again, Fritzi."

"Well, things started out real nice. He sang several songs to me. And—"

"Which songs?" Teddy interrupted to ask.

"Well, 'Jingle Bells' was one. Then you'd never believe the change that came over him. He acted so strangely I

164

almost expected to see him growing fangs."

"You're exactly right," Gram snorted. "I don't believe it. In fact, I don't believe anything you've said." She stomped from the room.

Fritzi's eyes met Teddy's. "She can deny it forever," she said softly, "but you're the one who's going to be saddled with him. Better watch it, kid. He's not normal."

"I'm going to bed," Teddy replied, her voice as raspy as Gram's. "We can talk tomorrow." She turned and ran through the door.

When Teddy passed Gram's open door she stopped and plopped down beside Gram on the edge of the bed. "What do you make of that?" she asked her dearest friend in the world.

"Bah! I don't make anything of it and you'd better not either. Fritzi probably jumped out of the sleigh at the end of our driveway and ran home so she could ruin your relationship with Brand. I've seen how cute she is around him. Haven't you?"

Teddy nodded. "But I didn't think anything of it. I figured that's how she treats men . . . all men."

Gram looked at her bedside clock. "We'd better hit the hay, kitten. Those fool llamas will think they're starving in a few hours. We can talk about this in the morning—if it's worth talking about. Good night." She gave Teddy a little push toward the door.

Don't we live a crazy life around here, Lord? Teddy asked silently as she lay on her bed in the dark. *Bless us and guide every move we make and even our thoughts so we'll be just what You want us to be and help us find out what happened tonight. Could You even help me forgive Brand for singing to Fritzi? Thank You, God. I love You.* She prayed longer, not asking for anything, just to be close to Him and savor His love and nearness.

The next morning she hopped out on the first peep of the alarm. She finished the morning chores, taking special care to check the young llamas, and headed for the house, feeling strong in the Lord. With Him she could handle anything.

Gram had breakfast on the table as usual but Fritzi had not put in an appearance yet. "Did you sleep?" Gram asked, looking very tired.

Teddy nodded. "Not too badly. Where's Fritzi?"

"Leave her alone," Gram grumbled. "Maybe she'll have a change of heart and tell us the truth."

Before they sat down to breakfast, the phone rang. Brand? "I'll get it," Gram said, rushing to the shrilling instrument.

"Tell him to come over," Teddy said just as Gram put the phone to her ear. After listening a moment Gram nodded at Teddy. "Teddy wants you to come over. Could you do that? Thanks, sonny." She jammed the receiver back on the phone. "He's coming."

Teddy ate a large bowl of oatmeal and a slice of toast. Then she started washing the few dishes in the sink wishing Brand would hurry and tell them what really happened the night before.

Brand did not execute his usual energetic attack on the front door, but opened it quietly and slipped inside. "I'm here, Gram," he called quietly. "I'm dumping my boots."

Then he strode into the kitchen, looking fresh, well rested, and happy. After washing his hands, he rubbed them together. He looked from Teddy to Gram. "I thought one of you were gone. Where's your little truck?"

Gram's bushy white eyebrows shot up. "Right where it

always is. I guess it's covered with snow. Are your eyes giving you trouble, Brand?"

He moved to the window. "I see tracks, Gram, but no red truck."

Teddy and Gram both dashed to the window and, sure enough, tracks led right past the house and down the driveway.

"Fritzi!" they yelled at the same time stampeding for her bedroom. They did not find Fritzi in her bedroom. Neither did they find any of her clothes nor the blankets, sheets, and pillows that had been on the bed.

"She's gone," Teddy said. "Why would she do that?"

"She decided the ranch was out of her reach," Brand said, "so she moved on, I guess."

The three looked in every corner and crevice of Fritzi's room but the woman had been thorough—nothing of value remained.

"Do you have a cup of coffee?" Brand finally asked, smiling at Teddy. "Personally, I'll feel more comfortable in the kitchen than in this room."

In the kitchen, Gram turned on the coffee. Brand dropped to the couch and motioned for Teddy to sit beside him. Somehow, having him there reassured Teddy. Soon, all sat around sipping the welcome, steaming brew. "Fritzi's leaving is for the best, you know," Brand said to Gram. "She'd never have been satisfied to fit in here."

"Oh, I know that, but we have to ask you a couple of questions, sonny. All right?"

"Of course. Just don't get on that tack Teddy was on for a while, wanting to know all the commandments I broke while growing up."

"Nope. This is now. Last night to be exact. Fritzi told us

you turned from Dr. Jekyll to Mr. Hyde—went stark raving mad—and threw her out of the sleigh into the snow, then whipped Thunder into a wild run getting away from her. That's what she said. What do you say?"

Brand set down his coffee, leaned his head back on the couch, and laughed. "Neither of you believed that, did you?"

Teddy shook her head. "No, but we could tell she had walked in the snow and we need to know what really happened."

"I hadn't planned to come home tattling like a little kid. But if you're sure you want me to. I didn't want to take her in the first place as you know, Teddy. I wanted to go to bed with our ride fresh in my mind. I was so exhilarated that I started telling Fritzi all about it. I even told her about singing to you, Teddy." He shook his head. "She told me she's closer to my age than Teddy, and would be much better for me. I tried to turn her off gently but she kept coming on to me— like a steam roller. Said Teddy's just a dumb kid and I'd get bored with her in a little while. Finally, I told her, in no uncertain terms, that I'd never be interested in her if we were stranded together on a deserted island." He nodded again. "That did it."

"I guess that was a relief," Gram said with a smile.

"Well, not too much. She stopped trying to kiss me and started trying to kill me. That's when it got tough. A guy can't hit a woman, you know, so I tried to protect myself somewhat without hurting her. Finally, she got tired of the whole thing, jumped out of the sleigh, and took off walking. I followed her half way and she told me to get lost."

"I should have known," Gram said. "I'd noticed her buddying up to you for some time now. I should have—"

Suddenly, although snow fell quietly on a still world, the

sun broke through and shone brightly in Teddy's heart. Brand had not sung to anyone but her! He had not sung to Fritzi!

Then a dreadful thought occurred to her. "Gram!" she yelled. "Do you have anything around that Fritzi could have stolen? I'll bet she knows exactly what's on the place."

Gram stopped short, rushed into her bedroom, and tore open the bottom drawer of her huge chest. They all saw the sagging door of the little fireproof box which had obviously been emptied. Gram turned to face the other two, her face pale. "Well, so much for all the cash we had around—close to $1,000, I think, and my only valuable jewel—my diamond wedding ring."

"Anything else?" Teddy asked.

"What about the deed to this place?" Brand asked.

"Oh yes, it was in there too." She wiped her forehead and sat down on the bed.

"Don't worry, Gram," Brand said. "That's why deeds are recorded at the court house. We'll just report it stolen."

Before the day ended they discovered Fritzi had taken Gram's heirloom silver flatware, three gold ingots, and several of Gram's handmade quilts.

"Are you going to report all this to the police?" Brand asked as he changed the outside door locks.

Gram laughed. "Naw," she boomed in her big voice. "Everyone's always telling me how much their kids beat them out of. Fritzi just takes hers in big bunches. Maybe she made me feel a little guilty, giving the ranch to Teddy. Not sorry, just guilty. Anyway, she cured my guilt."

Brand shook his head. "You're some lady, Gram."

That evening, Brand gathered Teddy into his arms. "I'm sorry our exquisite evening turned out so awful," he whispered into her ear. "We'll do it again and again, until we forget all about this."

Teddy pushed herself a little away from Brand so she could see him. "One more question. What did she whisper in your ear that convinced you to take her to Bend that night?"

"That? Oh, she said she wanted to buy you a wedding present. But she forgot all about it as soon as we left here. After that I knew she wasn't up to any good with me." He smiled ruefully.

"Let's try to forget we ever heard of her," Gram said.

The days went by and Brand tried to make Gram and Teddy truly forget the past few weeks. They rode horses almost every day. "You know Pharaoh's yours, don't you, Gram?" Brand said one day while they put the horses back in the barn and rubbed them down.

"Dear me, no," Gram rasped. "I couldn't take him from you. I do love him, though."

"He's yours, just as Misty's Teddy's. I'm glad for you to have him, Gram, because I'm so proud of the way you handle him."

The gruff old voice laughed happily. "We do get along, don't we? Thanks, son."

The snow melted, but returned a few days later, though not as deep. One morning, a fresh blanket of snow covered the roads, with light flakes still drifting down. Brand bundled Teddy into the warm sleigh blankets and took her out again.

"Where do you want to go?"

"I want to go into Bend." So they drove right through the center of town, Thunder's bells jingling all the way. People called out to them, laughing and throwing snowballs. Teddy waved, feeling happier than she ever had.

When they reached Teddy's driveway, Brand did not turn in, but directed Thunder on down the highway past his place. After a small effort to turn in, the horse seemed content to trot on into further isolation. Teddy and Brand sang together. They sang all the sleighing songs they both knew, then taught each other others.

Finally, Brand turned Thunder around and laid the reins at the edge of the sleigh. "Are you eager for Thanksgiving?" he asked. "And our wedding?" He cuddled her as close as possible with all their heavy winter clothes and warm blankets.

"Yes, it's only two weeks. Nearly everything is ready. The church people really took over the preparations. Gram is making the dress. Oh, Brand, it's so beautiful—and more so because she's doing it for me."

He reached a frosty mittened hand to her face and gently brushed a rosy cheek. "Did you know I love every little thing about you? Your bright blue eyes that reveal your whole being to the world. I love your innocence, I love your kindness . . . to Gram, to your animals, to me, and even to— that woman who wasn't very nice. I love your enthusiasm for your work and also for life. I love the way you love our Lord Jesus, and always talk to Him. Oh, Teddy Bear, our life is going to be heaven right here on this little earth."

Teddy lifted up a little and planted a kiss on his cold lips. "I love you so much I can't begin to tell you, Brand. I love you so much I touch your cup after you drink your coffee, and feel jealous because it touched your lips. Your golden hair and laughing brown eyes live in my every dream. Yes, I guess I'm eager for our wedding all right."

The harness bells had become still and Teddy came out of

her cocoon, expecting to find herself at Brand's barn, but Thunder had brought them to her ranch house. "He's getting smarter every day," Brand said chuckling as he guided her down from the sleigh.

Brand helped Teddy do her chores all the time now, leaving his to Rolf. Feeding, keeping plenty of fresh, unfrozen water available for the llamas, and making sure they were comfortable made up the bulk of the work now. "Aren't you glad we don't have to haul loads and loads of manure from the loafing sheds?" Teddy asked Brand with a wicked twinkle.

He shook his head. "Never quit, do you woman? Just don't tell Rolf that your llamas are housebroken; that's all I ask."

Brand took Teddy sleighing every time they had a fresh snow and she taught him to ice skate. They laughed over his clumsy first attempts to skate, but he learned quickly. Then she took him to Mount Bachelor where she taught him to ski. They went to several theater productions and an art show. And they entered Gram's new butterfly quilt in a quilt show.

Teddy and Brand spent nearly every waking hour together, doing something exciting, working, or doing nothing at all. Teddy's only desire was to be with him.

"Good thing you two are getting married next week," Gram said one evening. "It almost takes a stick of dynamite to get you apart these days. Not to mention the trouble I had finishing the wedding dress without you seeing it."

Brand agreed. "It's getting tough all right, Gram. One more week and we can be together all the time."

"Where?"

Two pairs of eyes watched Brand, waiting for an answer. "You know," he began, "I like your house a whole lot better than mine. Would you girls be terribly disappointed if we lived here? At least for a while?"

Happy smiles covered both faces. "I guess it's all right," he said. His brown eyes met Teddy's happy blue ones. "I'd live anywhere you want, you know."

"I know, and I feel the same way. You'll have to make the choice."

"Hey," he said, off on a new subject, "I read in the paper some dog sled races are starting from Bend tomorrow morning at six o'clock. Would you like to go watch them take off?"

Teddy wanted to go, so they got up extra early, finished the chores, ate Gram's buckwheat pancakes, and took off in Brand's pickup. In spite of the early hour, the large crowd provided a festive atmosphere. Vendors sold lots of hot coffee and sweet rolls; the harnessed dogs yapped their eagerness to hit the trail.

"What are they waiting for?" Teddy asked.

"I think they have a certain time to leave." He looked at his watch. "Didn't the paper say six o'clock? That's only five minutes away. Want some coffee?"

Teddy did not have time to answer for two men came up against Brand, turning him from the crowd. "Are you Brandon Sinclair?"

"Yes, I am. What can I do for you?"

"We'd like to ask you some questions, Mr. Sinclair. In fact, I have here a warrant for your arrest on suspicion of bank robbery."

nineteen

Brand's face blanched. "Bank robbery? What on God's wide earth are you talking about?"

The parka-enclosed man pulled a slip of paper from his pocket and read: *"You have the right to remain silent, Mr. Sinclair. If you give up that right, anything you say can and will be used against you in a court of law. You have the right to have a lawyer present during questioning, and if you can't afford one, the court will appoint one for you."*

Brand wrenched back from the officer. "Wait a minute. I haven't the foggiest idea what you're talking about, but you have the wrong man."

The officer looked at his warrant again. "Brandon J. Sinclair, 1234 Highway 20?"

Brand nodded, looking very puzzled. "That's my address, but I don't rob banks."

"Are you from Eugene?"

"Yes, but—"

"Come on, Mr. Sinclair, we can talk about it where it's a little warmer. Will you come willingly? Or do I need the cuffs?" He gave Brand a shove, but Brand put on his brakes and reached his right hand toward his pocket. The man knocked Brand's hand away from his pocket and handcuffed him so quickly Teddy almost missed seeing it happen. Then the man did a quick search of Brand but came up empty.

"You thought I was after a gun, didn't you?" Brand asked incredulously.

The man nodded. "The thought crossed my mind."

174

"Teddy," Brand said calmly, "would you get my keys out of my pocket and bring the pickup down to the station? We'll need it to drive home."

"Come on, Sinclair, we don't have all day. And you won't be going home for a while." Brand gave Teddy a small smile and walked away between the two police officers.

Teddy ran to the pickup and drove through the snowy streets to the police station. "I want to see Brand Sinclair," she said to the first uniform she saw inside the door.

The officer pointed toward the door. "You may as well go on back home, lady. Sinclair won't be receiving visitors today."

"But I have to help him."

He shook his head. "Somehow I don't think you're the right person to be helping him. You go home and come back tomorrow."

Suddenly, Teddy simply had to talk to Gram. "May I use a phone?"

He nodded toward a pay phone by the door and Teddy hurried toward it, eager to hear Gram's beautiful gravel voice.

"Why don't you do as the man says, kitten, and come home?" Gram suggested calmly when she had heard the news. "We can sort it out together."

Teddy drove as fast as she dared on the snowy highway. "What are we going to do, Gram?" she asked when she finally got home.

Gram settled Teddy onto the couch and put a mug of steaming coffee into her hands. Then she stirred her own and sat down in the rocker. "The officer was right, we can't help Brand. We can alert Rolf so he'll take over all the work over there. Otherwise. . . . Hey, I'll bet Lynden turned him in."

A frown creased Teddy's forehead. "Of course he did. I think I'll call him and tell him what I think of him."

"Better not. On the slight chance that he didn't, he's the last person we'd want to tell. I suppose it'll be in today's paper anyway, though."

The telephone rang and Teddy lifted the receiver. Brand's voice greeted her, and he sounded tired. "The Eugene police are coming for me in the morning," he said. "It's just as well. I'm as eager as they are to get to the bottom of this thing. Are you all right, Teddy Bear?"

"I'm all right. Brand, I'm going to Eugene, too."

"No! I want you to stay right where you are. Will you call Rolf and tell him he's in charge for a few days?"

"I already did. I'm going to Eugene, Brand. I have to."

"We won't get to see each other. It'll be a wasted trip."

"So it'll be a wasted trip. I've wasted things before."

"If you must go, be sure to stay with my folks. And tell them what's happened. They'll help."

Rolf readily agreed to care for the llamas while Teddy was away, so she left early the next morning. Driving over the treacherous winter roads in the icy mountains gave her little time to think about her wedding that was supposed to be less than a week away.

Could Brand be guilty of this crime? She had finally put it from her mind and now she must keep her faith. *But how could they have arrested him for something he did not do?* She knew Brand did not do it. *Had she not asked God to give her peace if everything was all right? And uncertainty if it was not?* She had never had one worry since that prayer. *If she could not trust the Lord, whom could she trust?*

Finally, about noon, she turned into Frank and Donna

Sinclair's driveway and pounded on the door. Frank opened the door and, seeing Teddy's grim face, helped her into the house.

"What's happened to Brand?" the older man asked, closely watching Teddy's face.

Teddy sniffed and swallowed hard, then pulled a tissue from her purse and wiped her nose. "He's all right. He hasn't been hurt or anything. Could we sit down, please?" When they all found seats, Teddy continued. "Please don't get excited, but Brand is in jail."

Frank burst out laughing. "What did he do now, rustle somebody's post holes so he could put them together and use them for a well?"

"No, they arrested him on suspicion of bank robbery."

Frank laughed even louder.

"Bank robbery?" Donna repeated. "He wouldn't even shoplift a candy bar."

"If he robbed a bank, he'd give it all to the poor, like Robin Hood," Frank said, starting up his loud laugh again.

"This isn't funny, Frank," Donna said. "Let's go to the police station."

They arrived at the station at almost the same time Brand did. Teddy's heart beat wildly when she saw the tall blond man. He had never looked more beautiful to her, though his ordeal showed on his face. The police let him hug his folks and kiss Teddy. "I love you." he said wearily. "We'll laugh about this in years to come when we tell our grandchildren." He gave her an extra squeeze and released her. "Somehow, it isn't all that funny right now."

"We're with you, son," Frank told him. "Surely they can't keep up a farce like this for long."

"They say there was one witness, the bank teller," Brand

explained. "They'll try to get her in this afternoon. When she sees I'm the wrong guy, that'll be the end of it. I took a polygraph in Bend. They wouldn't tell me how it came out but I've heard they're usually accurate. They also told me they've checked my pickup and it's exactly like the one used in the robbery, even the tires. Too bad they didn't get the license number." He looked at his folks. "If we could remember what we were doing the morning of May 2 it would help."

Brand and his parents hashed the date over for a while but none of them could come up with anything on that particular date. "Who's going to remember what they did at a certain time on a certain day seven months ago?" Frank asked.

"Can we be here when the woman comes in?" Teddy asked the officer.

"I'm not sure," the man said. "If you sit quietly over there by the wall they may not think about chasing you out."

Brand's parents and Teddy were allowed to wait with Brand until word came that the woman had arrived. The guard took Brand away, saying he would be back with a group of men. Teddy remained with Frank and Donna on a bench in the quiet corner.

After a half-hour wait, a woman walked in accompanied by a police officer. "You just sit here," he said to her, "and in a few minutes we'll have seven men come in and go to that center table. I'll be with them and make sure to talk to each of them. They know a witness is in the room but there are several other people too, so you watch and listen but don't say anything."

Teddy felt faint when the seven men, all tall, broad-shouldered, and blond, all dressed in dark slacks and light sweaters, came in. They walked around the room, close enough for Brand to give her the slightest wink. Then the police sergeant led them to the big round table in the center of the large room. They all sat down and talked for about fifteen minutes before the officer casually led the men out.

The man in blue returned almost immediately and pulled on his earlobe as he talked quietly to the woman. The little group, waiting so eagerly, could not hear the discussion.

After about half an hour, the woman left and the guards brought Brand back in. They all sat around the same table where the men had been. "The woman couldn't finger you," the man said. "She said she'd have thought any one of the seven did it if she'd seen only one. Your polygraph came out negative and we didn't find anything when we searched your place in Bend other than the pickup.

"We really don't have any reason to hold you longer. It appears to be simply a matter of coincidence, looking too much like the man who did it, and owning a matching rig. But I do wish you could come up with a solid alibi—just to close the case against you with 150 percent certainty."

Teddy looked into Brand's jumbo brown eyes and loved him more than she thought possible. How awful that he had been put through such an ordeal, and even worse that she had had moments of doubt.

Brand's wide smile reached almost to his ears, and his white teeth sparkled in the winter sun. "Let's get out of here." He held out his hand to the police officer. "No hard feelings," he said. "I want you to catch the guy as much as you do, but I sincerely hope I never have to go through something like this again."

Teddy and Brand stayed with his folks that night, so they could all travel back to Bend together for the wedding. After calling Gram, Teddy enjoyed staying up late with the family, talking about the ordeal they had just been through, then about the llama and cattle ranches and how Teddy and Brand planned to handle them both.

The next morning they all sat around relaxing and drinking coffee after a potato, ham, and egg breakfast, Teddy feeling secure in the crook of Brand's arm. "I know some people who'd be glad to stay in your house and help around the ranch for the rent," Frank said.

"Yeah? Who?"

Frank belched out a long jolly laugh. "Why Mother and I, of course. We're not only bored with city life, we're lonely for you."

Brand jumped up and cranked Frank's hand up and down. "Great, Dad. We'll be happy for you to stay as long as you like. The house will be taken care of, we'll all be together, and first thing you know, you'll have that grandchild you've been whining for."

The little caravan pulled into Gram's place at mid-afternoon and everyone stayed for supper. Before the evening meal, Brand managed to find Gram alone and suggested she call on him to ask the blessing for supper.

"You bet you can ask the blessing, son," Gram said. "Not only tonight but all the time. I'm glad to learn my boy's all grown up now."

Brand asked a special blessing on each member of the family gathered there that night—in a thoroughly adult way.

"Want to go for a ride?" he asked Teddy after they did the evening chores.

"Sure. Where we going?"

"I want to give Lynden a bad time for turning me in. Not that it was his fault."

They parked the pickup and walked into the newspaper

office where they found Lynden scribbling on a yellow pad. "I want a retraction put in the paper immediately," Brand ordered in a harsh voice.

Lynden looked up, surprise showing on his face, and scrambled to his feet. "Sure thing. You just tell me what this is about and I'll take care of it right away."

"You know what it's about!"

Lynden shook his head. "Sorry."

"My arrest for suspicion of bank robbery?"

Lynden's eyes opened wide. "You were arrested?"

"You bet, and spent two days and one night in the slammer."

Lynden tried to keep his mouth straight, but ended up unable to suppress a relieved smile. "I didn't report you, Sinclair, but I'm glad someone did. That's a serious crime."

"Who did report me then?"

Lynden shrugged. "I guess that's your problem." He picked up his black pen and started writing again.

Brand snatched Teddy's hand. "Let's go to the police station."

"I'd like to see the record of my arrest," he said, once they were inside the brick building. "I want to know who turned me in."

"Mr. Sinclair," the police officer began, "it was just rotten luck. Your description exactly fit the one given by the only witness and you also could easily be the guy in the bank picture." He shoved the pad to Brand and turned it around so he could see it.

Brand read a moment then turned to Teddy, pointing, "There it is, in black and white. *Fraedrick Marland*." He studied it another moment then raised his eyes to the man at the desk. "Can anyone turn anyone in for any old thing and get them into this much trouble?"

The man read a little farther. "Not just from a description, but this says the woman heard your girlfriend and her boyfriend talking about the crime, as if you had definitely done it." He looked up with a question in his eyes. "Your girlfriend has another boyfriend?"

Teddy almost stopped breathing.

Brand shook his head. "I'll be getting to the bottom of this." He turned Teddy toward the door and steered her outside into the snowy world.

"What was that all about?" he asked when they sat in the truck with the motor running and the heater going full blast. "I take it Greeley is the one Fritzi called your boyfriend. Did she make this up out of thin air or did she hear you two say something?" Then his eyes opened wide. "Teddy, did you know anything about this bank robbery?"

Teddy scrunched down in the seat and pulled her coat closer around her throat. "That's why I've been asking you personal questions," she mumbled. "Lynden brought me some items from the newspaper a few times and tried to tell me you did it. Then, when you refused to talk about it, I never felt quite sure."

Brand shoved it into reverse and backed out, then slammed on the brakes, killing the engine and sliding twenty feet across the icy snow. "I might be able to understand how you could believe something like that before you knew me, but how could have the faintest doubt later?" He started the truck again and headed gingerly toward home.

"I believed in you after I knew you," she said. "The night Fritzi was talking about, I told Lynden to get lost. She hid around the corner to listen and turned the story all around." She stopped and watched him, but he seemed to be concentrating on negotiating the icy road. She had to say one more thing. "But you never would tell me where you got the money for your ranch." She spoke in a whisper, then drew several small breaths. "Not even yet."

He glanced down at her and stopped the truck in the middle of the snowy road to take her into his arms. "You know what? The cops knew I'd paid cash for my ranch and they wanted to know where I got the money, too. They thought that was just too much coincidence. But I was able to prove I got the money legally. I should have told you long ago, love. The only excuse I have is that my folks believe strongly that it's in poor taste, even tacky, to reveal your financial prowess. I should have told you when we grew closer." His eyes grew misty. "But you should have told me about Fritzi too, you know."

He started the truck and explained to her as the pickup slowly found its way home. "My folks got nearly two million dollars for their ranch in Alvadore. They gave me about two-thirds of it. Said the ranch was more mine than theirs, as I'd worked so hard for so long." He drove a while then took her mittened hand. "It was sort of like Gram giving you her ranch, understand?"

She understood. Then she remembered the pickup. "How come you never drove the pickup anywhere? You drove it to my place and around on yours, but that's about it. A person could think you were hiding it."

He looked at her, a surprised look on his face, then burst into laughter. "Tell me, Teddy, would you drive that thing anywhere important? That rig's what I call a real bummer."

At last she understood it all. They hurried home to tell their folks what they had learned.

"Why should you be surprised?" Gram asked. "Fritzi

merely paid you for rejecting her advances."

"Guess what else we remembered while you were gone?" Frank said when a lull in the conversation allowed. "You didn't even own that pickup at the time of the bank robbery. It came as part of the equipment from the ranch. Now, if we could just remember what you were doing on the morning on May 2."

Brand nodded. "You're right. I'd never have bought a pile of junk like that. I should have remembered and told the police. Anyway, let's forget the whole thing and get on with our lives."

"You know what this all reminds me of," Teddy said, snuggling close to Brand. "All the time I kept telling myself I believed in Brand, I still had doubts. We do the same thing with God, know that? Whenever things don't go exactly as we think they should, we begin to doubt. I'm going to use this as a reminder to keep my faith in God no matter what."

"Right," Brand said. "I made lots of mistakes that caused you to doubt me but He never makes any. I hearby pledge to keep my faith too."

Three days later Teddy stood trembling in a small dressing room at the church. She pulled the lacy white creation over her head and watched breathlessly as it fell around her. Leaning over, she kissed the little gray head. "Thank you, Gram. It's the most beautiful wedding dress I've ever seen. And you're the most beautiful person in the world. I love you so much."

Gram, her mouth full of pins, kept adjusting the train. "Hold still, kitten. There, that looks right. I'm glad you like my work, Teddy, because I'm planning to make christening gowns for all of your babies."

Then Teddy found herself, on Frank's arm, walking down the aisle. Brand stood at the center front of the church, dressed in a white tuxedo, white frilly shirt, white cummerbund, and white bow tie. His sunstreaked hair lay combed back but rebelling here and there to fall over his ears. His brown eyes filled with love when he saw Teddy. He stepped forward on his long, long legs to accept her from his father. Teddy's heart felt full to bursting as he took her arm in his and turned to ascend the rostrum—to be together forever.

As they climbed the three steps, Teddy's eyes met those of her matron of honor—Gram. The old woman smiled happily and gave Teddy the thumbs up sign with both hands.

Teddy's eyes turned to Brand, who tightened his hold on her arm, gave her an almost imperceptible wink, then smiled broadly. Together, they faced the minister.

A Letter To Our Readers

Dear Reader:

In order that we might better contribute to your reading enjoyment, we would appreciate your taking a few minutes to respond to the following questions and return to:

Karen Carroll, Editor
Heartsong Presents
P.O. Box 719
Uhrichsville, Ohio 44683

1. Did you enjoy reading *Llama Lady*?
   ❑ Very much. I would like to see more books by this author!
   ❑ Moderately
   ❑ I would have enjoyed it more if

   _____

2. Where did you purchase this book?_____

   _____

3. What influenced your decision to purchase this book?
   ❑ Cover   ❑ Back cover copy
   ❑ Title   ❑ Friends
   ❑ Publicity   ❑ Other _____

4. Please rate the following elements from 1 (poor) to 10 (superior).
   - ❏ Heroine ❏ Plot
   - ❏ Hero ❏ Inspirational theme
   - ❏ Setting ❏ Secondary characters

5. What settings would you like to see in Heartsong Presents Books?

   _____

   _____

6. What are some inspirational themes you would like to see treated in future books?

   _____

   _____

7. Would you be interested in reading other Heartsong Presents Books?
   - ❏ Very interested
   - ❏ Moderately interested
   - ❏ Not interested

8. Please indicate your age range:
   - ❏ Under 18 ❏ 25-34 ❏ 46-55
   - ❏ 18-24 ❏ 35-45 ❏ Over 55

Name _____

Occupation _____

Address _____

City _____ State _____ Zip _____

LOVE A GREAT LOVE STORY?

Introducing Heartsong Presents —
Your Inspirational Book Club

Heartsong Presents Christian romance reader's service will provide you with four never before published romance titles each month! In fact, your books will be mailed to you at the same time advance copies are sent to book reviewers. You'll preview each of these new and unabridged books before they are released to the general public.

These books are filled with the kind of stories you have been longing for—stories of courtship, chivalry, honor, and virtue. Strong characters and riveting plot lines will make you want to read on and on. Romance is not dead, and each of these romantic tales will remind you that Christian faith is still the vital ingredient in an intimate relationship filled with true love and honest devotion.

Sign up today to receive your first set. Send no money now. We'll bill you only $9.97 post-paid with your shipment. Then every month you'll automatically receive the latest four "hot off the press" titles for the same low post-paid price of $9.97. That's a savings of 50% off the $4.95 cover price. When you consider the exaggerated shipping charges of other book clubs, your savings are even greater!

THERE IS NO RISK—you may cancel at any time without obligation. And if you aren't completely satisfied with any selection, return it for an immediate refund.

TO JOIN, just complete the coupon below, mail it today, and get ready for hours of wholesome entertainment every month.

Now you can curl up, relax, and enjoy some great reading full of the warmhearted spirit of romance.